Simply PLATONISH

PATRICIA MORENCY

Simply Platon-ish

written by
Patricia Morency

**Published by BlackGold Publishing, LLC in partnership with
The BlackGold Book League of Hampton Roads.**

1706 Todds Lane, Suite 258
Hampton, VA 23666

Edited by: Noelle B.
Designed by: John M.

First Edition: March 2023
Printed in the United States of America
ISBN: 978-1-953130-25-9

The views expressed in this book
are not necessarily those of the publisher.

Prologue:
Pia's Perspective

"Friendship vs. romance is a binary you can release if you want to. More queering of relational space; we've got a lot more than just two options." – Seher.

People like me exist, and we matter. *Read it again*. I felt I had to get that off my chest before we got started. This story is not for the faint of heart. No, it's not a story about murder. It's a story about race and gender. Ha, bet you wish it was about murder instead, *amirite*? Sorry, but I have a zero body count. This story is about Black people. I know. It's also a story about White people and privilege. Ugh, I know, I know.

Now, there may be quite a few of you who are already clenching your teeth. "Not another fucking story about racism! It's not all White people. I'm tired of feeling guilty for being White!"

If you think this tale intends to shame you, my dear White folk, then you are sorely mistaken. And it wouldn't benefit me to tell a story bashing White people. So let's skip past the white guilt trope, cause that's not my angle.

Whether we like it or not, our identities shape how we view the world and interact with one another. And I would be lying to myself if I did not acknowledge how the following events during my college years were influenced by the intersection of some of those identities, particularly gender and race.

Well, if it makes you feel better, this story centers on relationships. I will also say that unfortunately; this book does focus quite a bit on two women's conflict over a man. So basic, I know. But that's the surface. More deeply, it focuses on the

i

creating and unraveling of a relationship between a Black woman and a White woman. What? Layers, so many juicy layers.

Throughout this tale, you may hate one or more of these characters. But this story isn't meant to villainize one person over the other. We are all the unfortunate victims of injustice, whether we are Black or White, men or women. And I'm only focusing on two categories: Black/White and men/women (pardon the binary lens). In this particular story, no one is the hero, and no one is the villain. We were all victims of patriarchal supremacy, creating a restrictive narrative of love, romance, and friendship, manipulating our insecurities within them.

There, I said it. White patriarchal supremacy: the system that dictates what we can and cannot do, should or should not say, love, or should not love.

That is the only time I'm gonna say it. **Maybe**.

I hope we can take a collective breath and lean into this story. You really gotta roll with the punches on this one, White folks. There's going to be shit in here that may confuse you, intrigue you, and piss you off. I hope you mindfully notice when you feel uncomfortable or upset when something happens to one or more of these characters. Lean into it, but do not let it pull you into emotional paralysis. Learn and move on. My BIPGM (Black, Indigenous, People of the Global Majority) friends, take a seat back and enjoy this wild-ass ride.

This story is more than just complications and tensions in the relationships of these three main characters. It's more about missed opportunities and the pain caused by societal expectations and norms of friendship, romance, conflict, forgiveness, and communication. And these societal expectations further complicated and destroyed two relationships that could have been meaningful and lasted a lifetime.

So there you have it.

A good experience with this book would most likely involve you hating me at multiple points throughout this story. A great experience would involve you getting around to liking me again eventually. Not that I care.

Many of my peers wondered over the years about the nature of our -three-way relationship. I never knew what to say. Fuck labels. But if anyone asks me now...

I'd say it was simply platon-*ish*.

Chapter One // How to Survive a College Reunion that *Never* Happened

hate myself for being here. I *really* do. Just look at me, my pathetic little self-sitting here all alone on a Friday night, just feeling miserable and shitty. *Why did I have to go? Why did I have to attend that reunion?* Nope, nope. I'm not going to do that to myself. I am not going to beat myself up for going. I thought it was amazing. 99% of the time I spent there was amazing. It was perfect. But those last two minutes, that is 1% of the time. Ah, it just fucked me up.

Hold up, sorry. Let me back it up and introduce myself. Hello, my name is Pia, and I'm a sexless Jezebel who is in love with a married man.

Wait, that's not true. *Why would I start like that? Why would I say that about myself?*

But there's one true thing. Ethan and Jacq are married. To each other. *What the actual fuck.*

Oh. No. Why am I feeling bad for myself? No, I decided to go to that reunion. *Well, was it actually a reunion?* During a year of so many losses and changes, this was another one. A reunion that was supposed to be large and lavish was reduced to yet another week of computer screens with people in tiny boxes. Nevertheless, I was inclined to go and reconnect with people and a past life I yearned to relive.

And to reconnect the past with my progress since then. I am proud of who I have become over these past ten years. I've gotten more degrees. I'm doing great work. I love my coworkers. Sometimes. I like who I am. *So why do I feel terrible?* I am a fucking cliche. A heartbroken woman who clings to the romanticized version of the past. Like an urban romantic dramedy from the nineties. The scorned Black woman trope.

No. I'm not making any sense. I'm the cool non-jealous intersectional feminist, a down-to-earth and easygoing person. Single. *A badass.* Not thinking about getting married and having kids. Yet. Maybe. I'm okay with where I am in my life.

I can't be jealous. In graduate school, I learned about compersion, the idea of feeling happy for a partner getting some of their needs met through someone else. While it was in the context of polyamorous relationships, the concept highlighted a deeper meaning for me. The broader theme of interpersonal relationships: being non-possessive and understanding that one person cannot meet all of someone's needs. I thought it would be liberating to practice this concept in all types of relationships. *So why do I feel so terrible?*

I take a moment with the question. Oh, God. The realization hits me like a ton of bricks. *I'm in love with a married man. Oh, my Caribbean parents would be so proud.*

He wasn't married when I knew him. But he was in a relationship. And was it truly love, or something else? I thought I got over these feelings. I thought that I had moved on. So why the fuck do I care that Ethan married Jacqueline?

And they weren't even there at the reunion. That's the worst part: to hear that offhanded yet heartbreaking comment from a mutual friend, Ashley, during the last two minutes of our virtual reunion.

"Well, it looks like the lovebirds couldn't make it tonight. Hope they're enjoying married life in quarantine."

"Who are you talking about?"

"Ethan and Jacq, who else? I emailed her about the reunion last week, but she never responded."

Typical Jacq, I thought.

"But wait, what? I stumbled, jumbling my words. They're mar...?"

I could barely get the words out before the video meeting disconnected. No time to process it, to ask more

2

questions. It threw me off. And now I'm here feeling sad and confused.

I thought maybe they'd gone their separate ways or met other people and got married. I had no idea. This brought back so many memories. Why did it have to be that way? Sheesh! No, I must admit to myself that there was a tiny, maybe not-so-tiny part of me that thought that maybe I'd run into them separately. They were no longer together, and they were single, especially Ethan. And maybe we could have started talking again, and there could have been something…a renewed and mended friendship, or…No I can't even think about that now. I can't think about that now.

I'm not going to beat myself up.

You must be so confused right now. You deserve an explanation as to how terrible I feel. We were all friends, the three of us, since our first year in college. How the hell would we know how things were going to turn out? That those two would start dating each other. That I would stay friends with both as a couple for all those years. That some things may or may not have bubbled up from underneath the surface. My being the recipient of not-so-direct accusations and feeling guilty somewhere down the line. I thought I buried this a long time ago.

Maybe I need to revisit this. After all, it did affect me. It still affects me, now. Before I get into it, I will acknowledge that I might sound a little contradictory to the statements I made earlier.

Some days, I feel like I got my shit together. I think I'm above and beyond this. I feel like I've forgiven myself. Days where there is no self-blame, and I think of myself as a good person. And then some days are like today. This night after the end of a 10-year reunion, I feel like a terrible person. And these negative and irrational thoughts, or maybe they are rational thoughts…Nope, I'm doing it again. These irrational thoughts keep popping up in my head and I just question who I was back then.

Oh, I remember myself back then.

I have not changed that much in terms of the essential parts of myself that I love. But I was going through some things when I was younger. You know, maybe I should take a step back. I gotta take a step back and let y'all know what I'm talking about. Maybe it'll be good for me to just revisit this and put it to bed. Well, if I'm going to start this at the true beginning, I guess it starts in my first year. Day 1 of the first 40 nights that would change my life.

Chapter Two // The Day I *Almost* Fought a Tall-Ash Nerd at Graduation

By the time I got to college, I was a firecracker. I was the person that was like, "Don't nobody start nothing. I am who I am and I don't give a damn! You either with me or against me, ho!" It is interesting thinking about it right now and realizing that I never really told my friends about it, especially in college, the things that happened to me before I remember distinctly making a promise to myself starting college that I wanted to make a fresh start. I wanted a complete reset.

So as I sat in that gymnasium during the first full night at college, filled with screaming teens in brightly colored shirts representing our dorms like sports teams, I breathed deeply and soaked it all in... Maybe this could be great. Maybe this could be my new home? It was hard to think positively so soon. But something inside me felt like soaring when I saw people's faces light up when they saw me. A new friend. Another person who can share this once-in-a-lifetime experience. The first night of college. A new beginning.

Then I remembered: this was the first time I sat in a large area with people since my high school graduation. A day that did not go as well as I had planned. And the first and only time I almost got into a physical altercation, in front of hundreds of people, no less.

I know that a lot of people are afraid to leave their hometowns and go somewhere completely new, let alone far away, for college. It is a very scary thing because there are a lot of unknowns, and you don't know if you'll be accepted. I can understand that. But for me, it was the complete opposite. I was so, so happy to have a fresh start in a completely

5

different place where no one knew me. I was not as concerned about reinventing myself but more excited to freely embrace my authentic self regardless of what others thought of me. And I was happy to find a place where I knew I would be accepted for who I am. This was the enticing, seductive part of the experience that just drew me in.

I thought this way going into college due to a long history of being bullied and ostracized for being different. I marched to the beat of my drum, kept my head in my books, and did not go out of my way to fit in with others. And that pissed quite a few people off. Which is a long, complicated story that goes back to my childhood. But the one thing that I would say that put the icing on the cake for me to be like, "fuck this, I'm moving away and going off to college," was my high school graduation.

So picture this. It's June 2007, the last week of school, and graduation is only a couple of days away. During that week, seniors had a bunch of activities that led up to graduation. Well, after our graduation practice one morning, we were able to leave school early. But when you dismiss a bunch of high-schoolers early, there are bound to be many people sticking around. It was also the day we got our yearbooks, so people were staying behind to sign each other's yearbooks and pictures to reminisce. That shit.

I never bothered to buy a yearbook. I did not want to have it at all. Why did I need another reminder of the last four years in a place that I genuinely did not like? I do admit that I was active in certain activities. I was a nerd in the advanced courses, and after school, I was part of the musical theatre crowd. Even though I was part of those groups, I still didn't feel like I completely fit in. Though I could not put it into words at the time, I knew on a subconscious level there were different ways to be a nerd and a theatre geek, and they were all legitimate ways of being a young person. But for some reason, it felt like people had to fit a certain mold or version of those identities to be accepted.

I had already gone through years of being bullied in primary school for being smart, quiet, and obedient to a fault. Granted, my thirst for knowledge made me a know-it-all to my peers. My crippling anxiety made me outwardly appear curt when speaking publicly instead of what I was inside: insecure and afraid of failure. My perfectionism made me engage in ritualistic behaviors such as double-checking agendas and assignments, which made me appear annoying to students and teachers alike. My fierce obedience to authority and need for rules and structure made me "adultified" and more out of touch with my childhood peers.

That was the part in which I struggled the most. It wasn't just the obedience to authority, even though that was a major factor. I was taught from home that children were supposed to obey their elders and whoever was in charge, regardless of what other people thought. If other people were in line themselves, they would also understand the importance of conceding to authority. Even when they disagreed, even if the authority was wrong. It was not my right as a child to question them. Although, as a teen and adult, I began to question some things in subtle and sometimes not-so-subtle ways. But that was much later.

I know I am not the only person who grew up with internalized authoritarian beliefs. However, there is a particular downside that no one talks about, at least in cases similar to mine. And I am not talking about the parents' unrealistic expectations or even the pressure to succeed and the negative impact on self-esteem. Those effects primarily focus on the parent-child relationship. What about the impact of that behavioral pattern on a child's peers? Classmates and peers do not like a goodie-two-shoes or a teacher's pet. I had an additional, complementary personality trait that created another barrier between my peers and me. I had a strong, independent moral code beyond the influence of my peers.

First, let's just set aside the content of the moral code itself. I don't need to go into specifics to illustrate the devastating cost of this independent way of thinking. Just imagine the idea of having a distinct set of morals that you would follow regardless of other people's morals and beliefs. Now in an ideal scenario, if your morals and values were in line with folks around you, then that would be great, right? You would behave similarly to your peers and there would be group harmony. But that's an ideal scenario. In reality, there would be times when the values are in sync and other times when there are not. And the crucial part is how you behave and communicate those differences with your peers. However, if you happen to be vocal about how your morals are different and do not even try to follow the crowd, guess what happens?

My mind since I was a child was constantly processing and exploring the world in different and often imaginable ways. Because of this, I guess I developed my core beliefs, tastes, and interests earlier than many folks my age. And they were so firmly planted in my mind and integrated into my character that I felt completely justified and secure in those aspects of myself. I didn't need to fit in or please others to help shape my identity by comparison; it was already pretty much formed. People do not like when someone marches to their own beat and doesn't follow the crowd, especially if they are unapologetic about it. But that's the problem that I never knew I had. I somehow internalized the belief that it is okay to openly disagree with the majority, to follow my own thoughts, and most importantly, not change for the sake of group harmony. To not change for the sake of following my peers and fitting in. I only had to change for authority. The authority figure's beliefs and rules were the things I had to conform to for the sake of group harmony. With peers, I felt free to openly disagree and be different because I had the understanding that having different opinions and not conforming shouldn't damage a relationship.

And by the time I was in high school, I still did not fit in with a crowd, making matters worse for me. I still did not find my #squadgoals, a group where I could just be me. I usually had to justify the way I thought and believed: I wouldn't pretend to like the drama director to get a lead role in the play; she was a mean and controlling hypocrite. I wouldn't pretend to like sports when I was confused by them or wear pretty pink dresses and high-heeled shoes just because they were in style. They hurt like hell, no matter how much a short person needs them. And I wouldn't take someone insulting me lying down, no matter how popular they were. And past bullying lowered my trust levels in people while heightening my apathy toward them. Trauma will do that to any bitch, for real. I honestly believed for a long time that people were incapable of genuinely loving and caring for others, and that belief extended to me. Towards the end of high school, I became more comfortable with being a loner than changing parts of my personality to better fit into cliques.

So back to the day before graduation. Following graduation practice, I stuck around to chat with some friends. I was wrapping things up and about to go home when this one classmate started storming in my direction. I knew this person for a while at this point, but not too well. We had been in some honors and advanced placement classes since sophomore year. She rushes toward me with a scowl on her face and her yearbook clenched in her hand. She stops inches from my face, and in front of a crowd of at least forty people, she shouts, "You fucking cocksucker!"

No shade to people who engage in this activity. I did not know the term "sex-positive" at that point in my life, and I did not harbor harsh feelings towards people who had sex, even oral sex, with others at our age... I even remember being mad that she was trying to shame me in front of all those people with that word.

Then she pointed to the section of the yearbook listing the class officers. It was well known that she was our class secretary. However, instead of her name and picture being in that spot, there was my name and picture. When I looked at my glossy image, I was just as confused as she was. I had no idea how my name and the picture got put in her spot. She continued to yell at me, blaming me for what she thought was some sort of trick that I played with my fellow friend and yearbook editor.

I did not do this, and I am sure to this day that she probably still would not believe me. That day she was pissed off, looking ready to fight. I was not in the mood to fight. So I walked away and headed home.

I thought that was the end of it. But the next day, our graduation day, all the seniors went to this restaurant nearby for our senior picnic. I distinctly remember getting a ride with a classmate who loudly blasted music. The ride was so short she only got through half a song. But it was a good one: "On the Hotline" by the Hip-Hop/R&B sensation Pretty Ricky. I remember being somewhat bashful while the music blared so loudly in the parking lot, with all its glorious and sexually explicit lyrics. But we were almost out of high school, baby, and I loved it so much!

The beginning of my love of hoe music.

I was having a decent time chilling out with people at the picnic, listening to school-sanctioned radio music in the wings. I didn't even notice her in the background. You know who I'm talking about. Once again, I didn't want to deal with it. So I headed home again. When I got home, I decided to tell my parents what was going on. They were just as confused as I was.

I went to the graduation ceremony that evening, waiting patiently in a crowd of 600 students to hear my name. My last name is Marcelle, so I had to wait a while. That year, the front row was reserved for our class officers, which included the class secretary.

After an hour of waiting in my aisle, they finally called our row. I took a deep breath, thinking, "I can't wait to get out of this place. Let's GO! I'm done, I'm done, I'm done." After an hour, they finally called our row. I took a deep breath, thinking, "I can't wait to get out of this place. I can't wait to get out of this place! Let's GO! I'm done, I'm done, I'm done." I walked up to the front, and the presenter called my name. I took another deep breath. *Sweet, sweet victory*. The end was so close! I shook their hand, grabbed the diploma, and started to walk towards the photographer at the end of the stage.

Then it happened. Behind me, I heard snickering. Then a female voice said loudly, "WOOHOO! Give it up for the class secretary!"

That comment pissed me off. Admittedly, it was a mild statement, barely an insult. Another time, I wouldn't have given it the time of day. However, this was my special day. Until that comment, I completely forgot about the high school drama. I was finally at peace, excited for the future, and no longer depressed or anxious about existing. With that simple bullshit comment, she just ruined the one moment of peace that I had.

I don't know what came over me, but I was so pissed. Then I acted completely out of character. That peaceful obedient,

11

nonviolent student was filled with rage. I pivoted towards her, the diploma holder in my left hand. Then I flipped her off in front of the whole front row. There were some loud gasps. Quite a few of the White students clutched their pearls in disbelief and shock. Even my parents, who were way in the back, saw it. But somehow, all the teachers and the other officiants didn't see it. Or maybe they pretended not to see it.

Five quick seconds of glory. I walked off and sat back in my row seat. I quietly waited the remaining forty or so minutes for the ceremony to be over. It finally wrapped up, and the students dispersed readily, to get their real diplomas at assigned tables. I stayed with my friends talking about what just happened. I was about to say bye to my family and head off to celebrate with friends. Then this blur comes charging towards me, angry AF.

I should disclose that there was a significant height difference between the two of us. My little short-ass is five foot two on a good day. I guess I cannot say specifically how tall she was. For a frame of reference, my father is five foot nine, and she towered OVER him as she walked past to get to me. A giant woman in heels.

She stopped a couple of feet in front of me and said, "Oh, you think you're clever now, bitch, flipping me off in front of all those people!" Fighting stance initiated. I threw my hands up in the air. Fuck it! I graduated. What else are they gonna do? They can't kick me out of school. I'm done!

And as I was about to pounce, my father walked up to me from the side. He said gently, "It's not worth it." I don't know what Caribbean voodoo magic spell he cast on me, but that immediately snapped me out of my anger, and I just walked away.

But I think I surprised myself with how angry I was on that graduation night. And I subconsciously brought that

12

apathetic energy into my freshman year of college, which expressed itself in interesting ways.

On the other side, I also began to cherish and embrace that dominant masculine side of myself. And that did kind of set me up for success in terms of being authentically and unapologetically me.

Returning mentally to the gymnasium of my freshman convocation, I realized another layer to my approach to college. People walk into college having expectations, but the truth is, you can never really know what college life is unless you've been through it. And no one in my immediate surroundings knew about university life since I was the first in my family to go there. So I would be remiss if I did not acknowledge that other layer to this story. What I will say foremost is that being unaware of the college norms and rules can become a breeding ground for creativity: making your own rules, challenging the traditional ways of cultivating interpersonal relationships, and flourishing while living in the margins. It can also be a complete shitshow, a hilariously ignorant stumblefuck.

How did this happen?

Well, let's start with my odd yet basic immigrant family background.

Chapter 3 // Second-Gen Earnest, First-Gen Ignorance

My family and I had no clue what college was about. But we tried anyway. We never got a chance to say goodbye during that first day of orientation. I was unexpectedly swept away by the large crowds of freshmen, chanting the songs of their dorms as they marched into the gymnasium for our convocation. Everything happened so fast that all we had time for was a quick *bisou* before I was literally carried away by the crowd. But I wasn't too scared. This was the moment my family and I had waited for, and we were confident that I would do fine. Maybe too confident.

Let me take a step back here and introduce you to my roots.

So I come from a Caribbean, Afro-Latin family background, and I was the first person in my family to attend a four-year college. Both my mother and father emigrated to the country in the early 80s, on separate boats, as we would joke to ourselves. My mother was still finishing high school. My father had started college but transferred to a technical school where he got licensed to do engineering-type work. I honestly still don't know what he does to this day, and he has been at the same job for over 20 years. Okay, I know about sixty percent: enough to introduce him to new people but not nearly enough to explain the fantastical world of operational engineering. Can you blame me? Folks expect me to memorize thousands of books' worth of material since elementary school, get perfect grades, stay up-to-date on current events, AND remember my parents' professions... Parents can dream, but they can't get all three. And if they had to choose between those options, they would agree with my decision.

I cannot stress enough the sheer importance of education in my family, hell, my entire culture. There is some truth to the saying that Caribbeans only praise educational achievements. It took me a long time to learn that other children in other cultures (e.g. White kids) were praised for personality characteristics and other benign things. Don't get me wrong, my parents always told me that they were happy and content with my work as long as I tried my best. So when they learned in first grade that my best work resulted in straight A's, I was screwed from that point forward.

Although none of us at this point in my life had attended a four-year program through university, there were certain things that my parents and I understood about education. The most important was its value in attaining the American Dream. Ah yes, the immigrant parent's dream that burdened their second-gen kids' backs. I knew from a very young age that I needed to have an education. I needed to do very well in school, and anything less than an "A" was considered as failing. I was the first child, and the expectations were very high. They instilled the value of independent hard work throughout my childhood. Seriously, I was almost today years old when I found out that most 7-year-olds did not spend their weekends completing the next week's assignments ahead of time.

Before anyone gets agitated, I must say that I truly do appreciate how seriously my parents took the value of education since they instilled in me the ability to be a self-starter and complete tasks independently. They always told me if I was unfamiliar with a concept, I should teach myself. This skill came in handy when I had to apply for colleges and explore topics that I was interested in but instructors did not have the time or interest in teaching me.

Interestingly, as I look back, I also think about the conversations that my parents had with me leading up to my going away to college. My parents did want me to enjoy the new environment and make friends, but it should only be the backdrop to succeeding academically. My parents were also pro-sex and anti-drinking. Quite the interesting combo, I know! They were very against my drinking before I was 21. No matter how many 80s party movies they loved watching with

15

me, I was not allowed to partake in those festivities until I was of age. However, fun fact: for my 15th birthday my father gifted me the DVD, **American Pie 3**. His coworker loaned him the movie, and my birthday was that weekend, so there you go. My parents and I watched the movie together, and my father was laughing harder than anyone, especially during the assless chaps scene. Even though my parents came from a historically conservative and religious cultural background, they were surprisingly sex-positive and liberal. So I watched rated R movies with them as a teenager, and my mother had open sex-ed conversations with me to fact-check the content we watched. I will say that while both my parents were open and tried to normalize the concept of sexuality from a developmental standpoint, there were a couple of times when my father's beliefs and behavioral patterns were contradictory in the most hilarious way. The same person who gave me a raunchy comedy as a 15-year-old forbade me to listen to the Bootylicious album just a few years earlier. This is slightly related but tangential: in college, I started to watch adult animated comedies with my much younger sister. One day my father was using our larger desktop computer in the basement while we were watching an episode. The male child character was wearing a dress and shouting the word "vagina" repeatedly as he was talking to an old man who I assume was Dick Cheney.

Wink if you know what I'm talking about.

Anyway, my father is typing away in silence as the boy continues to say that word a billion times. Then all of the sudden, the older character says something along the lines of *"Shut up or I'm gonna kick your ass,"* and my father suddenly swings around in his chair and says sternly but confusingly;

"What the heck are you watching? Change the channel." So, to make this clear, he had no problems with the word vagina, but the word "ass" was too much for him to handle. Do you see what I mean? His thought patterns and actions weirdly do sort of make sense, but at the same time, I often wonder how this can all be the same person. But I digress.

It was never explicitly stated, but the expectation was that I wait until after high school to start having sex. There was never an issue of my waiting until marriage, only until I was "old enough." I guess it also helped that I was not actively seeking relationships or sex during high school anyway.

However, when I visited my school of choice for the first time, it was a refreshingly different experience. It was so amazing, y'all. It was like a fairy tale. My father accompanied me on the trip. They had separate schedules for the parents and the students. I had an overnight host, and she was a freshman. She was Black, surprise, surprise. It was a good thing we matched, to get that shared identity experience, but still, it was obvious they matched all of us based on race.

The campus and people were very down-to-earth, and the schedules for that weekend were organized to a tee. The leadership team thought about everything. We had no complaints. It was amazing, and I was able in that short amount of time to talk to people and get a sense of what types of activities and groups they had. I didn't know what to do with these unexpected, positive emotions. But the environment intrigued me and relaxed me to the point that I began to look forward to my first year.

My dad was at that point the sole provider in our home. So I knew that I had to get a scholarship to help pay for myself, so I applied to all of them. When I first got accepted, I got a considerable amount of money. It was the type of amount that was significant but also made us feel bad for our situation because it still was not enough for us to feel truly comfortable. And I remember I had a chance to visit the school's financial advisor before I enrolled. I don't know if the financial advisor saw the appreciative yet subtle concern on our faces

17

reviewing my financial aid package.   We were polite and nodding, but I guess the advisor could still see the wheels turning, thinking about how to make up the gap in aid. Within a week after we left, we had an updated financial aid package containing additional funds. Holy shit. They read our minds and the deepness of our souls. I felt like Cinderella. So after that, I was like, "*Yes, this is where I want to be.*"

There was one other thing that I remember from that trip. It was a comment made by my overnight host. I asked her about making friends and hanging out with new people. At the time, I was attending a high school that was very racially diverse. I think it was about 60% White and 40% People of Color in my neighborhood. And there were significant numbers of people of Filipino and Indian descent, along with Hispanic/Latinx people and African immigrants. But it wasn't until I went to high school that I was around many White people, and I became very comfortable hanging out with them. So fast forward to the last night of this college visit. We're having a conversation, and this first-year assumed I would only be interested in Black Student Union and hanging around Black folks. When I asked why she was only mentioning Black folks, she responded it was the main way I would socialize in school. That did not sit well with me, but I moved on because I simply did not believe her. That's your experience, I thought. Not mine.

I became even more invested in making friends with people of all different races. I was not planning to stick to just Black folk. I should admit another reason behind my feeling triggered at that moment. Although I essentially grew up in a predominantly Black neighborhood, and as you can recall, I was not treated in the best way. Fuck it, let's just call it for what it was: I was bullied mostly by Black folks, although not exclusively, as I grew up. I guess I would be lying if I did not acknowledge how it impacted my sense of connection towards the Black community. I felt this fear that if I were to continue with exclusively Black folks, I could run the risk of being bullied again for my "White" characteristics: nerdy,

18

serious about studying, never socializing, mainly getting high grades, etc. But ultimately, I think there was part of me that internalized the negative social history with Black peers but not to the point that I believe that all of them are bad. Still, I was adamant about opening up to having meaningful relationships with people of all different races, including White people. Not to mention I knew that it was a predominantly White campus, so chances of running into them and connecting were highly likely.

Thinking back, I wonder what life would have been like if I had chosen to be more intentional and connect with my Black roots, to fully engage in all the different activities and social groups from the motherland at my new school. Afro Pick in the hair, waving my power-fist in the air like I just don't care... *Clearly*, I had no clue where to start. However, I still love the decision that I made because it brought me down a path that was awkward and unapologetically me at the time. I acknowledge this is not, for lack of a better term, a Black and White issue. I do not believe I needed to choose one group over another. And I did spend much time with Black folks throughout college. But I mostly spent time with those I lived with, and they were White. (Were White? **Are** White? They did not change colors, to my knowledge.) Also, I was at a point in my life development where White folks had not damaged me so completely that I ran back to my Black roots with arms wide open, seeking respite and refuge. (That didn't happen until years later, she says as she's wearing a garment from her Black AF collection...)

But when it came to making friends in general, my family and I still had no freaking clue. The social component of life is so vital to one's well-being and growth as a person. And I think my lack of awareness, particularly the cultural and social conventions as to who to hang out with and what to do, was kind of a blessing. Because if I had learned the American standards and rules of social engagement, particularly regarding gender and race, I probably would have been much more self-conscious and I would not have made the bold moves I did, which at that time I did not know were bold. I would have not been able to make the moves that challenged and flipped the interpersonal world upside down. I also was in an environment where people didn't give me that feedback. They did not say, "This isn't how people typically behave" or "These aren't the choices that people typically make in regards to making friends." Or even how to behave as a woman on campus, let alone a Black woman on campus.

So: as much as my parents were critical about that study life and adamant about my not drinking as it would deter me from success, our collective lack of awareness set the tone for me to make crazy-ass moves according to American standards. Thinking about that, I laugh because if we had taken a course on how to engage with American college students beforehand, I wouldn't have been able to have the best experience I had. So there you go with that.

Chapter 4 // Love is a Second-Hand Emotion

"**H**ey boys!" I shouted confidently across the quad as I spotted a couple of tall white male students. Convocation just ended, and I was looking for people to walk back to my dorm, my new home.

New home. That sounded weird to say.

"Wait up!" I said, running up to their group. They happened to live on the same floor as me. "Wow, that was some event tonight!!"

We already semi-met each other during a quick floor meeting that day. They smiled at me, and we all proceeded to walk back to our dorm, continuing to ask each other get-to-know-you questions. I felt comfortable with them. We were just talking, nothing else on the table. I guess that was how I viewed these types of things. *Nothing to worry about here.* It didn't cross my mind to be self-conscious about this group of boys. It wasn't like I was trying to cuff them or get them to fall in love with me. *Can you imagine that? Ha!* I couldn't. It never was on my radar.

For the longest time, I've had a very strange relationship with love. I did not believe in the concept of love, or more specifically, romantic love. I was familiar with the love that one has for one's family and blood relatives. I got that. I understood that. But I did not understand how much people obsessed over this vague idea of romantic love: the crazy type of love that caused people to do ridiculous things. I very strongly did not believe it truly existed.

I firmly believed that the love that one sees so often in movies and TV and what people write romantic love songs about was just that: it was for the media. It was a fairytale. It was a snapshot, a perfect-world scenario. When I consumed this type of media, I did it with the knowledge of knowing that it was imaginary. It wasn't something that could actually happen.

I bet you would probably think that I kept this opinion to myself. But no, I remember very openly and candidly expressing my opinions about this throughout high school and thinking that it was pretty normal to do so. Or I should say it is common to do so. It's hard to believe that someone intellectual, perhaps mature for her age, could have such a staunch and negative outlook on life. But it was true. And I think it's because I had seen and experienced such horrible treatment from people, and I lived in environments within a society where I felt like people did not know how to treat each other well. People treated each other poorly to the point it was expected. At school, on the road, at work, at the supermarket checkout line, and more. I just felt like we as humans could not truly care for one another, in such a selfless way. There is a memorable quote from the movie *Crash:* "It's the sense of touch. In any real city, you walk, you know? You brush past people; people bump into you. In L.A., nobody touches you. We're always behind this metal and glass. I think we miss that touch so much that we crash into each other, just so we can feel something."

That was the way I felt about love: that was just simply an illusion, fostered by a chemical imbalance. A need to squelch the numbness we felt as we concurrently and selfishly interacted with each other in such cruel ways. I did not exclude myself from the group and from that need. I never thought I was above those feelings of numbness within a world of cruelty. I acknowledged that I responded to cruelty with cruelty and self-hatred myself. I tried to drive that bad energy inward, but I knew it spilled out from time to time. How else could someone cope with negativity directed toward them without reflecting it on the world?

I also believed that sex was just a recreational activity for pleasure. And something that society also tied very closely to the concept of love, even if it was not present during the moment. Another reason that I didn't think this kind of transcendent, romantic, selfless love existed was that, on the other hand, it felt like it was driven purely by a desire for sexual gratification. So, people duped themselves into believing that they fell in love when they just wanted to have sex, and they used that as a way to justify their feelings. I could have sex with someone right now because I think I'm in love, and you're supposed to wait until you're in love to have sex. Women were especially fed that script. And I remember actively challenging that idea by thinking that if someone wants to engage in sex purely for pleasure, that is fun on its own. Why try to justify it by pretending that you are in love? It reminded me of the story Romeo and Juliet, which was one of the main reasons why I didn't like it. I believed that Romeo and Juliet was just a story of horny teenagers that made up this belief that they were in love, so they could justify getting married and fucking each other at a young age. They could have just spared all the pain and the suffering if they had just had sex and skipped all this bullshit and flowery language and courtship and all that stuff.

So I thought of love being an imaginary story, a lie that people tell themselves. And I often thought to myself, "let's just cut the bullshit and go straight to the sex." According to my internalized family beliefs, it wasn't a matter of waiting until marriage for me. It was more like waiting until you're old enough, whatever old enough meant. The closer I got to that idea of being old enough, the more I was excited to just get it over with and do it because I wanted to. And it would be more satisfying to do it that way.

I almost engaged in sex during the long weekend of my prospective freshmen orientation. It happened a month after I had gotten accepted. The invitation came with my acceptance letter. I was low-key annoyed that it was prefaced as a multicultural event, as if to say, "Yay, you got in because of affirmative action." Not that affirmative action was a bad thing. Well, in theory. Years later, I would learn that the policy most benefited White women, which was the group that I least pictured when I thought about that concept. Anyway, I digress.

I was a bit skeptical about going to the event in the first place. But as soon as I got off that plane, I was captivated by its beauty and grace. And during that short amount of time, I was able to connect with some people. And I met someone I found interesting that weekend. His name was Tomas. Yeah, that name sounds as hot as he was. On the last night, we were hanging out together at the dance they planned for us, and it turned out to be an inadvertent date. Before that night, I didn't imagine myself hooking up with him or hooking up at all, but as the night progressed, it seemed like people started pairing off. He was hanging out with me more. We danced all night. After it was over, we walked into each other's dorms. And it felt like it was just the two of us against the world. And I thought, *hey, this is such a perfect place in time to just do it. I found someone that was interesting enough for me to consider having sex with. I had a good time. It's a long weekend, and I probably won't see him again. If I did ever see him again, that's great; but if I didn't, it would be a great time to think fondly of.*

I *almost* went through with it. If it wasn't for another person cock-blocking me. It was one of his friends, a male friend. Now, I'm not trying to justify my sexist bias, but it was not the stereotypical person you would think who would do this to me. But his friend came over, pulling Tomas to hang out with him instead. If that damn person was not there, I probably would have invited Tomas to my temporary dorm for the weekend to do God-knows-what. I would say that my interest was piqued rather than me having a full-on attraction to him. Not to say I had no sexual interest at all; It was just the first time I could see myself eventually having sex with him if we talked more that night. But it didn't happen.

Anywho, that was one of many examples I can think of that showed how loosely I was tied to sex. It wasn't something that I felt needed an emotional attachment, just some sort of interest. I admired people who engage in sex that way, with no love attachment. I think it is a very positive way to do it, and people can have sex for many different reasons other than love. That's fun, and that's okay.

When I started my college journey, I still had these very firm beliefs that love wasn't something that would exist in my world. For me, it was not an option. I could see myself hooking up with people, maybe even having a causal relationship, but it wasn't something that was a priority for me, and love was not part of that equation. I was also very academically minded, especially during my first year. I was on the scholarship, y'all, and I wasn't going to mess that up, especially for love.

I felt so fortunate to be accepted to this magical place that I did not want to do anything to fuck it up, let alone get into some random relationship with somebody. I did not want to get caught up in my feelings and have that ruin my ability to get a good grade and keep my scholarship. Can you imagine the shame for me and my family? That was the furthest thing from my mind. I would have had a better chance of being caught with drugs. Starting college, I distinctly remember being like, I don't even want to have a relationship because I don't want anything to ruin this opportunity.

Additionally, when I saw people in love, I saw people giving up their careers, autonomy, sense of self, and judgment. It was for the other person for the sake of themselves. It wasn't just the idea of caring for someone because it's cool to be supportive of someone. But caring for someone so much that you put yourself lower than them? That was some shit that didn't fly for me. And like I said, I never really had that deep feeling for love. And my sexual attraction to others was fleeting at best and not oriented anywhere. But it was a better course to follow than love. I remember thinking maybe this person might be someone that I would want to fuck, someday. But to have a lovey-dovey, hold your hand, stare into each other's eyes, lay down on the beach, looking at the stars sharing a blanket, type of love. It was just a fairy tale that wasn't for me.

So what happened during college that fucked up all those aforementioned notions for me? It wasn't something that struck me right away. It was a slow process. And it was a process that involved meeting different people and imagining new and different ways of connecting with folks. And it all started the night after freshman convocation.

Chapter Five // Rude Gyal Banter

I know that I'm a sexy bitch, thank you. I get the sense that I may have given you the wrong impression. Sometimes when I talk about my beliefs on love, I get an eerie feeling that there are people out there who think I have a low self-image.

> "She only thinks this way because she thinks she's not beautiful. Love yourself!" Fake-ass Karen squeals to me.

Let's be clear: I didn't have perfect self-esteem, but it wasn't low either. I knew I was attractive at that time. It was a matter of whose gaze we were talking about here. I knew I wasn't the standard of beauty, the one that people immediately think about when they picture a hot young person. And fuck yeah, it had to do with race.

I wasn't a tall white supermodel, the first draft pick. If you catch my drift. It used to annoy me, but I coped by knowing it was a systematic problem. I would often joke as if it was a matter of food preference. Cheeseburgers and sushi may taste good, but most people reach for the cheeseburger first. People aren't going to go for sushi unless they've learned about it before or lived in an area where they were already familiar with how good sushi was. *Get it*?

And for that reason, I came to the hard but true belief that other genders, especially those outside my race, would not find me attractive. Or I should say, they may find me attractive but wouldn't go out of their way to pick me out in a sea full of blondes. You would think that would depress me, and deep down, it probably did more than I thought, but I mostly found it liberating. I didn't have the pressure of feeling sexualized or the need to impress people. I could just exist and be with them and have honest conversations without the fluff of trying to impress me to get into my pants. So I felt comfortable saying whatever the fuck I wanted to, whether or not it sounded unladylike or shocking for someone who looked like me. Because of this, I often had fun with vulgar language and crude sexual jokes. Why not? If the joke fits.

I also never thought that my comments about sex were highly sexual. I felt comfortable talking about sex with people, even men, and most frequently around them. And because I never thought of myself as a sexual object to them, I never thought that my comments could be construed as flirting. This is something I learned years later. Like MANY years later. Reunion night, actually, lol. I considered it to be just banter. You know, casual conversation. Anyway, as I got back to the dorm after convocation with my boy band of a crew looking like their backstage manager, those vulgar and blunt comments started slowly coming as we talked through the night. Side note: we later made a quote wall on our floor, which had a lot of submissions from me.

Also, it is important to know that I have a great and rare ability to have sexual conversations with other genders, feel empowered, and not desire to have sex with them. We could talk about sex explicitly, even about each other, but for me to think of engaging in sex at that moment? Uh, no! That's weird. Don't see the connection there.

I used to think I felt sexually gratified when I did it, but now I realize it was more like empowerment or playfulness. There was no real agenda for me, other than seeing if other people connected with my personality and interests. I realize that thought process and experience is rare now as I look back, but at that time and for the longest time, I didn't think it was odd or special. I thought it was common and that many other people did it as well. Little did I know that I was conversing in ways with folks that they have never experienced before, especially from a woman. I was more into building deep connections through complex conversations about sexuality instead of flirting to get someone's attention or start a relationship. Women don't do that type of stuff in college, right? Bat an eye, touch a shoulder, and compliment a man to catch a dick? Right? That's only in the movies, right? Shit, was I wrong!

Chapter Six // Meeting Ethan

I hung out with many tall White men, especially during my freshman year. Of course, that isn't a unique experience for most people, given the American college landscape, which is majority White. And as you may recall, I broke my White social group virginity in high school, which is later in life for many people. However, in college, I had my first experience of being the only Black person in groups of White folks. Unlike many other Black folks around a sea of white people, I was not entirely uncomfortable. I knew I stood out, for sure, but I got a bit used to being around White folks starting in high school, where my social circles were more racially mixed. I used the term "social" lightly since it was more like iterating with people in the classroom and the lunchroom. I rarely if ever had true friends whom I would socialize with outside the classroom. I never had the *Friends* or the *Saved By Bell* social experiences that I thought were standard for friendships.

Especially after our convocation, I became low-key fascinated with learning more about my White peers. One of the main concerns I had with starting college was not having much in common with my peers, whom I assumed came from a higher economic background. I was right about part of it: many students who went to my school came from at least upper-middle-class backgrounds, and most of their parents had attended four-year colleges themselves. I thought most of my peers would be rich, spoiled, and materially obsessed. I was afraid that I would not be able to spend time with them because they would be interested in activities or items that I did not have the money for to engage with them. Fortunately, I was mistaken. For the most part, the folks that I spent time with liked the same types of activities, and they were all about sales and finding the best deals. A sweet situation for me. The surprising part I did not account for was the free and simplistic activities they enjoyed and how interested they were in having me spend time with them.

I assumed I would eat alone during the first few days of college. I was fine with that--after all, I did not know anybody to dine with. Yup, I was wrong about that. That seems like something I should be excited about, which I was deep down, but the initial request took me by surprise. Once again, this may appear to be indicative of someone with low self-esteem, but that wasn't it. As someone with my particular set of identities, I was used to being ignored in public spaces. So when a tall White man knocked on my door that first night after orientation, I was a bit shook.

I remember it quite well. It was close to dinner time and my roommate and I were in our dorm room getting ready for our separate plans. She already had a group of friends for her dinner plans, and I was trying to remember all my options for food spots. I opened it and saw a tall, pale, gentle face with a smile.

"*Hi*," he said.

"Hi," I said back, slightly confused.

Why was he here? Was he looking for my roommate?

"Did you get dinner yet? We've been going around the floor seeing if people want to go out with us." I peeked behind him and saw a couple of people waving back at me.

"Thanks for the invite, but I already got people I'm going with," my roommate said.

"Okay, cool..." He turned from her and looked at me.

"What about *you*?"

"Oh… um, yeah. Sounds good." I said sheepishly.

"Great!" He smiled. "Meet us in the common room in five minutes?"

"Yeah, sure," I responded. "Um, sorry. I know we hung out after convocation, but what is your name again?"

"It's Robert."

"Nice to meet you again, Robert. I'm Pia."

Robert had an interesting personality. He was the type of person that could start a conversation with anyone. He did a great job bringing different groups of people together, which was great for us first-years who struggled through awkward ice-breaker conversations. Starting that night, and every night afterward for the next several weeks, Robert would knock on the different doors throughout the floor and gather people to go to dinner on campus. I became part of the core group with him every time. Because of him, I got to meet with many of my floor mates. I felt completely out of place the first few times since I had not been to many hangouts, especially this often. When I was in musical theatre in high school, we would go to the local diner every once in a while. But it was a pattern of once every couple of months if that. I started to go out every single night with different folks as we tried to find our core friend groups. Now, I did not know this was happening, that people were also using this time to find their squads. I just went in with the idea of it being a routine, and it did not matter to me that much who was coming as long as I had Robert with me. He, in many ways, was the glue that kept the socializing together.

Slowly over time, fewer new people showed up to our mini floor dinners, and more of the same folks showed up consistently. I still had somewhat of a hard time remembering names. This is going to sound terrible, but there were quite a few tall White guys that I kept mixing up. Facepalm. It was like a revolving Ferris wheel of White dudes, and the game was to learn their names and personalities. Gosh, I wish I could tell you I was deeply invested in remembering people's faces and names, but I wasn't, at least in the beginning. I was more into picking up vibes. This may be why it took me a while to truly notice the other people who would eventually become part of my group. It did help that the numbers slowly came down, and there were about five or six of us who started to have dinner regularly.

In the revolving door of White men who came through my life during those first few months (phrased like I had a good ol' time being a hoe, but alas, y'all know that's not what I meant), there was a particular person who was always hanging around in the background. He wasn't too shy, but he wasn't too talkative either. He was congenial and had a quiet simple demeanor that I found unintimidating. I hate to say this, but I often forgot he was there. But also sensed he was always there. Not in a creepy way, but in a calm, pleasant way. He never really dominated the conversation and would typically go with the flow of the crowd. *If only I could remember his name! Fuuuuuuck.*

It took me about a couple of days to catch folks trying to say his name so I could finally commit it to memory. This was also when he began to share more stories and bond with Robert. They started to do a bit together, creating these what-if scenarios, and adding more ridiculous details with each comment. And it all was done in a dry, sarcastic tone. It took me a while to learn that they got their inspiration from Abbott and Costello and, more importantly, the Monty Python TV series and movie franchise. Don't worry if you're not White and don't know who Monty Python is. You're not missing much; it's just your standard British humor that I assumed people of color never found funny. That was the belief I had at the time.

"You don't find it funny because you don't get the meaning behind the joke," they often told me.

"No, I got the joke. I just don't find it funny." I would say, matter-of-factly.

For future reference, let's just assume all my statements were said matter-of-factly. I often made those types of comments, not out of rudeness or intentional

33

rudeness. That's just how I spoke. It was blunt and honest, and at the time, I did not realize how uncharacteristic it was for folks, White people especially, to be in the presence of a woman who constantly spoke that way. Straightforward, with a fresh seasoning of vulgarity.

"Well, you gotta watch more of their comedy to understand British humor better," Robert said. "Me and Ethan have been watching their movies since we were kids and we love it."

Ethan! That's his name! Eternal sigh of relief.

In case you are wondering, it was not always just me and a bunch of dudes. Ah, a sweet paradise that would be. Okay, I'm just kidding. But I would be lying if I didn't admit that I liked the company of male friends more than women. And most of my life had been surrounded by women as friends. Some okay, some decent, and some not-so-great. It was refreshing to get the chance to spend more time with men. But it was always a mixed group in terms of gender. As our floormates groups got smaller and we melted into standard cliques, there was one woman on the floor who also began to spend more time with us.

I hung out with this woman before, within this group, and outside the group with other female floor mates. She became part of the girl group that would take trips to Target together. Like Ethan, she wasn't as talkative, but I did not believe she was shy. It just felt like she did not have as many stories she wanted to share as others. More of a listener, like me.

The first interesting story I remembered about her happened during one of our Target outings. I think they all had the same class or something like that.

"So it was an interesting time we had last night, right Jacq?" our mutual floormate said.

"Yeah, I guess so, Amy."

"Now that I think about it, I think Jordan *really* likes you. He keeps trying to hang out with you."

"Yeah."

Who the hell was Jordan? I had no clue. He was not on our floor; I knew that for sure. A normal person would have asked for clarification, but this seemed like a one-on-one conversation that I should be publicly eavesdropping on. After all, I was standing and walking right next to them. They knew I was there.

"So, what happened? I saw Jordan trying to talk to you on the side, and then you two walked away." Amy was curious about the deets. And so was I, a little bit.

"Oh, well, he kissed me," Jacq replied in a calm, mild tone. One would say, almost matter-of-fact.

"What?" Amy squealed. "What did you do?"

"I kissed him back."

"Oh, WOW!" Amy exclaimed.

This was some interesting tea. I wasn't quite as excited as Amy, but I was intrigued by how Jacq was explaining this story. I got the sense that she didn't truly like him, but I didn't quite understand why she would kiss him back. It didn't seem like he forced her to do it or that she was mad that he kissed her, but she didn't appear to like it. It sounded like a script that she felt she had to follow. I felt completely disconnected from and confused by that logic. I didn't have much experience in that department, so I couldn't judge. Outwardly. Inside, I was like, *Why?*

What is even more interesting about that story was that I never heard about Jordan again. For the rest of college and beyond. I'm pretty sure he continued to exist as a person, but at least not in our lives. Or the part of my floor mates' lives that overlapped with mine.

Chapter Seven // We Be Up All Night...Talking?!

The great part about college is that socializing doesn't stop at dinner. Often I would spend long hours with my floor mates through the night. The first time I started spending the whole night with them, I did not know what to expect. Well, maybe I had a few thoughts swirling in my mind. I did believe for a second that if I stayed up with them long enough, it would turn into an orgy. And depending on my mood, I would join out of sheer opportunity and curiosity. There was maybe a hint of desire but more of a fascination from an outsider's perspective. Sorry to burst anyone's bubble, but there was never an orgy. Well, I never ended up in an orgy situation. My freshman roommate supposedly ended up in an orgy in a different room during our last night of freshman year, and I am still upset to this day that she did not invite me. That should be a second-tier running theme for this book…

No, instead of the night turning into something pornographic, all we did was spend the night playing games and talking. I was not aware of this White ritual: late-night talks. If anything, I thought it was a hilarious joke I heard on some show at some point in my life. But sure enough, there I was, chatting it up with these White folks until the break of dawn. Like, who does that? Apparently, **I did**. Beyoncé would be ashamed. This is not what she meant when she said in that song "We be up all night!" I did feel awkward in the beginning and felt cheated. *We are young. Heartache to heartache. We stand. No promises, no demands. Let's fuck on this battlefield.* I think that's how the song goes.

I wasn't sure if I would engage in the group sex scenario I had in my head, but I was curious enough to watch it. Oh, come on! Like you never thought of it. I wished more movies focused on the technical aspects of lovemaking. Laying down on the mat the selection of lube, the assortment of condoms, and other methods of STI and pregnancy prevention. Doing stretches to get ready like we're back in high school gym class. Figuring out positions like a game of Twister. Everybody wins! But nope, none of that happened. The closest I got was getting all the boys to take their shirts off one night during an almost game of strip poker a couple of years later. But as fast as the shirts came off, they went back on. They liked the idea but were not comfortable going through with it. I get it; good times can't be forced, and enthusiastic consent is always sexy.

So, back to late-night chatting. Slowly but surely, I grew to appreciate this once-believed to be an outdated art form. I became more comfortable as my squad shared their background, life stories, hobbies, and interests. It turned out that Ethan and I had a lot of things in common. First of all, there were the understated similarities: both from the east coast, considered ourselves liberal, not deeply religious, and took our education seriously (i.e. nerds). These were the factors that were so base-level minimum requirements for friendship that I didn't even give it a second thought. There was a major, unprecedented election during our freshman year, with the assumption we all liked and would vote for the same person. We were in favor of social change and progressive values. Once again, it was basic stuff that I never considered to be a luxury to find. I expected the people I was around to share those values. (Later on, living in conservative states broke me out of that reality *real* fast).

For example, we had some similar interests in music. I always liked listening to different music genres, but I'd be lying if I didn't admit to being a basic millennial who most often listened to Top 40 pop. Still, I did enjoy listening to rock music and Classic 80's jams as well. I became an absolute fan of Green Day when their album *American Idiot* was released while I was in high school, as I deeply identified with the loner walking on the "Boulevard of Broken Dreams." I took pleasure in exploring other types of music, like a treasure hunt of eclectic tastes. Ethan and I bonded over our love for Maroon

5 as he shared their first album with me, something that I was interested in procuring but never got around to since hearing "This Love" for the first time in middle school. He also introduced me to the Red Hot Chili Peppers. I was familiar with their recent song "Dani California" at the time but did not know any of their other songs. I also learned about the simplistic beauty of Regina Specktor and the playfulness of Ben Folds. Ethan shared his collection of selected songs from years past, and I listened to all their songs with piqued curiosity. I liked how varied the songs were in terms of genre and composition. They were rock but not rock, and their beats were easy to listen to on walks and long drives. Every time Ethan shared a new song with me, it was like getting another glimpse into his personality. I felt our bond got deeper the first time we discovered a mutual interest in a song in real time. As we watched *The Thomas Crown Affair*, a first for me, we both smiled at each other when we took note of the smooth deep tone of the singer's voice in the song "Oh Sinnerman" that played throughout the film. It was a different tone and texture that intrigued both of us, a combination of African and jazz cadence.

That memory distinctly came back to my mind one time after college when I first heard the theme song from the show *Suits*, similar texture and deep tone. I wonder if he watched that show too...

One night, I walked into the common room and saw a movie on the big screen that I had not seen since childhood. It was one of my favorite movies, but I never knew anyone my age who also purposely watched it. It was the 1980s sci-fi comedy *Spaceballs.* And before you start calling me old, I just have to say that you are...right. It was already a classic by the time I was in middle school, let alone college. But I was an old soul who had always been into oldies and classics. So I sat down that night in the common room, quiet, interest piqued. During one scene, I mumbled the word "jam" right before the radar in the spaceship was covered in grapey gooeyness.

"Oh, you've seen this movie before?"

"Yeah, I've watched this a bunch of times growing up."

"Mm-hm," Ethan said affirmatively, not out of disbelief, but more like he appreciated our common taste in movies.

"Use the Schwartz!"

From that point forward, I watched other Mel Brooks movies and other classics such as *Young Frankenstein,* the *Princess Bride,* and *Robin Hood: Men in Tights*. Then one night, Ethan and I watched *"Blazing Saddles."* Yeesh.

Or I should say that I walked into Ethan and other floor mates watching *Blazing Saddles.* If you haven't heard of that movie, please do a quick Google search before proceeding. It was made in the 1970s, but that's not an excuse for what I'm about to share. I will admit, I can appreciate, to a certain extent, the humor and genre of the film. I am a fan of dark comedies and satires and enjoy messed-up jokes, especially those related to social commentary.

I realized then and now that Blazing Saddles is just that: a dark comedy satire poking fun at the systemic racism and history of oppression in the Old West. You never see Black cowboys on television, even though there is a rich cultural history of African American cowboys and horsemen, a fact that I did not learn until I saw an episode of *Braxton Family Values* that took place in Wyoming in 2018. The premise of Blazing Saddles was that a new sheriff was in town, and he was Black. It was shocking to the White folks in town, and they (un)shockingly had an issue with it.

I don't remember most details of the movie. The most salient thing I remember was part of the movie that I walked in on. As I walked into the dark common room, I saw a bunch of White cowboys on the TV shouting the word *nigger* on screen. Repeatedly. Mockingly.

"What the hell is this?" I asked, super confused.

"No, no you're seeing this out of context. This is a comedy."

"Really?"

"Yeah, it'll make sense when you watch it."

"Okay," I said as I sat down on the couch.

And I did see the rest of the movie. And I remember it did make sense to me. The White folks were speaking the way they would about Black folks during that time, very openly in public. And the Black sheriff did end up getting his revenge on those folks. Once again, I can see how it was a social commentary on how White people underestimated Black professionalism and excellence. And how this Black man used that to his advantage and showed all of them just how great he could be as a leader. But the way I was introduced to that film, sheesh! I tried to be open-minded since it was another Mel Brooks movie and I thought he could do no wrong. That's a weird statement to hear from a Black millennial, right? That an old White man can do no wrong? Okay, it's not just me.

On the flip side, we did end up watching the *40-Year-Old Virgin* together, and I remember my White peers getting very quiet during the scene where Kevin Hart had a back-and-forth with another Black man in which they said the N-word fifty billion times. I watched this movie before with my family, and we laughed our asses off when that scene came up. But this time, I got nervous around my White friends. I could not bring myself to laugh the way I did around Black people.

You may be thinking, "Well, yeah, it's because you were in a room with White people." And yes, that is true. But it was not the first time I watched or listened to something that had that word in front of White people my age. There were plenty of times in high school I listened and danced to uncensored rap music. They played uncensored music at my school dances. It did not make me uncomfortable until I came to college.

Oh, speaking about that, Ethan had a very strong opinion about the rap music genre. He even borrowed an old-timer's quote to summarize it: "Rap is Crap!" I was disheartened to hear this opinion. I am a firm believer that music can bring people together, and I loved it when he introduced me to new types of music. Each new artist or genre was a new piece to the complex puzzle of global consciousness. It was something reflective of a person's soul and character and those who were similar to them. Looking back now, that was probably one of the reasons I began to fall in love with him, through the activity of sharing music. But I did not notice then.

However, as much as I cared about the music he shared with me, to the point that I respectfully listened to all of it, he got upset every time a song came on that sounded remotely like rap. He would complain and say that it was not real music. This was another time when he had what I would consider "good reasons" behind his beliefs, but deep down it still ticked me off, and I could not find a way to articulate why. He said that he could not listen to a genre of music that was materialistic and oppressive to women. *Damn it! Case and point*. He wasn't wrong: many rappers have songs that talk about all the money they have and all the cars and houses they got. And no one can ignore the hyper-sexualization and exploitation of women in those videos. Because of those reasons, I felt that I had to agree with and respect his beliefs. But I did not appreciate how he kept complaining whenever a rap song would play around us. It didn't matter if I was playing it, or if we heard it on the radio, or as we were walking through campus. I did continue to play my music, however, and I argued with him until I switched it to my headphones.

Well, there was one time that I could not contain my anger for much longer. Ah, yes. I remember it clearly. A bunch of us made a glorious trip to procure some frozen custard. I was super excited since the place we went to was a major staple in the region. We gleefully headed back to the car, our stomachs full of sugary goodness, and a new song started to play on the radio. It barely played, like three words. It was

OMG by Usher, and before Will.i.am could get the words "Oh my God" out, Ethan let out a major sigh.

"Ugh," he sneered in discontent. "Can we change the station?"

That was it. I had it. The song didn't even play for a few seconds, and he couldn't handle it. But this seemed over the top, even for him. We only heard the sound of someone's voice, and it was enough to irk him.

Then I said, without hesitation, "Why do you always get upset whenever you hear a Black person on the radio?" *Oh, shit.*

I had a weird dual sensation at the time. There was a strong part of me that did not understand how harsh and direct that statement was. For me, it was just a comment I made based on what I saw. The song only played long enough for us to realize it was a Black artist, and it upset him. So logically, I thought my interpretation was on point. It was not as much an accusation but a genuine inquiry about his snap judgment. On the other hand, it was an accusation, and I even questioned whether or not I said that comment aloud. I still question myself sometimes today. But what followed was confirmation that it happened.

Out of the corner of my eye, the two other people of color (nonblack) gave each other a look like, "Did this trick just say that? Damn, that's bold!"

After a beat of silence, Ethan replied. "No, it's not that. I just really don't like that kind of music."

"Uhh!" I huffed, but I stopped myself from going further in exhaustion. I thought the conversation was going nowhere, so what's the point?

"You can leave it on," he said in a quieter tone.

"Alright..." Our RA said awkwardly, as she backed the car out of the parking lot.

Oh yeah, did I forget to mention t our resident advisor was there? Yup, another person of color. I think she had that "damn she's bold" look as well...

What was frustrating during those times was I felt something flawed in his logic, but I could not identify it. I knew there had to be more to the story, of why people seemed to be so focused on the debauchery of rap music compared to other genres. And I had a feeling that rap was not the only genre of music that had those flaws. (It was not; I confirmed later. I'm looking at you, rock music.) I also had a problem with his positionality on the matter, but I could not completely understand why. Now I understand that it troubled me to see a White person as an outsider have a moral objection to a genre that put him on a superior level in terms of taste. Ugh, if only I trusted myself to engage in those intuitions and had that lexicon to back it up! And it may be just me, but whenever I'm in an argument of differences with White folks, I feel the pressure to back up my statements with research and cited references. Why did I feel pressure to have research to back up my beliefs? People should be able to take my word as enough, without me having to cite a study, which would only confirm my knowledge and experiences. (and if you don't believe in me, there's a term for that: worship of the written word[1]. Fuck, I did it again!)

First of all, if other genres are also materialistic and oppressive to women (I'm looking at you, country music), why do we as a society solely put the negative focus on the one dominated by Black folks? And I knew deep in my bones that rap music was a rebellion against the mainstream and a place for Black folks to create and celebrate aspects of life that were truly theirs.

This feeling resurfaced when Miley Cyrus briefly entered the rap game, only to abandon it for the same reasons Ethan said years before. However, I don't think it's fair for a

---

[1] "Worship of the Written Word" (.whitesupremacyculture.info/worship-of-written-word.html)

White person who is removed from the culture to dip their toe in it or state their opinions on it in a way that asserts some moral superiority to the creators within the genre. Look, y'all are not model citizens either. And let's not forget about Black women in the rap genre who are creatively responsible for their hits and embrace sexuality to the point that they openly celebrate it. Is it fair to criticize them if they are not oppressed?

I never had the chance to get Ethan's opinion on that particular matter, but I could see him thinking it was tasteless, especially since it is not the societal norm in society for women to be that sexual. Or should I say intelligent, confident, and sexual? It felt at that time, and even today, that a woman has to choose between the two: either intelligent and not hypersexual, or dumb and hypersexual, as if to say that only unintelligent people would choose to flaunt themselves that way. What I now understand more clearly is that folks have a hard time with the marginalized owning their sexuality as power. It is a power of enormous, autonomous proportions that the non-marginalized cannot control. It is also a self-sustaining source of pleasure that scares the shit out of folks who have been in control and take pleasure in regulating the actions of others. White culture has had a dulling and suppressive effect on human behaviors in society. People cannot be emotional in public. Women must keep harmony and maintain peace even if there is disagreement. The ultimate role of women is a caregiver and pacifier, dependent on someone else for pleasure and security. Sexual power stands in direct opposition to this, and it is seen as a threat even if it is not meant to.[2]

Sure, Ethan had good intentions behind his beliefs. He came from an upbringing that valued women's intelligence,

---

[2] The Power of Dance As a Mental Health Tool for Women | Shape: shape.com/lifestyle/mind-and-body/mental-health/black-women-dance-mental-health. This article discusses the history of twerk as a meaning of healing and liberation, and the negative connotation of Black women twerking.

independence, and the right to their bodies and sexuality. I don't believe he was against premarital sex or pro-choice. I don't think he would post social media comments shaming women for engaging in hypersexual behavior, whatever the hell that is. I've been using the word hypersexual, but what does that mean? What's the line between sexual and hypersexual?

Anyway, Ethan also was (and probably still is) anti-social media. He never liked it or was active on it. Trust me. I am not trying to make a case for him or make excuses for his problematic beliefs. What I do want to emphasize is how shockingly normal his beliefs are, especially among White liberals. Does that make them terrible, irredeemable people? Debates commence! And I can't believe I have to say this, but y'all probably got the sense at this point that I'm not conservative, right? I'm talking about my people here. Well, you know what I mean.

Sexual power isn't something to be accepted with exceptions. It is messy as it is beautiful and unique in its strength and liberation. Oftentimes, we hear of liberal folks stating that they are fans of women owning their sexuality, but for many, it is often really up until a certain point. If you think about it, there is a line that if crossed, will trigger their defenses *real* quick. How far is too far for folks? Sometimes it is not as far as people say it is. This is most evident when sexuality is present or shown in environments where it's frowned upon. A woman can dance sexy in the club, as long as the sexiness stays there in that one place. But if at work it is found that she listens to raunchy music on the regular or goes to sex dungeons on the weekends, she is looked at differently with contempt and discomfort. It varies in intensity but there nonetheless.

It is also holding the view that sexuality would somehow leak into professional spaces and make people uncomfortable, and damage others in the inherent purity of that public space. And I'm not talking about overt sexuality in spaces meant for children. This view still holds in many adult-

46

dominated spaces. And when it comes to the adult woman persona, if she maintains her sexy side while being a single woman, not in a rush to get married or have kids, then she is considered dangerous. Why? The problem is that it is an unfair, unrealistic, and limiting view of sexuality to hold as an oppressive force over people. A professor can also be a burlesque performer/stripper, and a mental health therapist can also be a twerker. I use these as examples of real people.

I am also fully aware of the particular hyper-sexualization and eroticism that is part of misogynoir. Many colleagues in the field (Audre Lorde, bell hooks, Patricia Hill Collins) have written about how Black woman's sexuality has been perverted, subjugated, and co-opted for consumption by the White gaze. Any attempts to self-embrace it in liberation would be subversive.[3] Yet, I still believe a person should be fully accepted in terms of their sexuality and sensuality, however pervasive it is within themselves and their personality and however it is expressed out into the world (bell hooks). And I am defining sexuality to primarily mean freedom of expression and way of being, which is inclusive of things outside of sex. What? Did I just blow your mind? What were you thinking I was talking about this whole time? Therein lies the problem.

So while liberal-minded folks may believe they are acting out of moral interest and concern for those involved, particularly in the regulation of sexuality in certain spaces, they are truly missing the point. First, it is not meant for their consumption, and second, it alludes to the manipulative nature of stable romantic relationships, and the societal norms of how a woman should behave once she is at a certain age and within a certain long-term relationship. And this has everything to do with music since the lyrics reflect life embracing sexuality. Something that should not be shunned, especially by those people outside of its walls. Our history and

---

[3] Existence as Resistance: How Josephine Baker Challenged Misogynoir (lithub.com/existence-as-resistance-how-josephine-baker-challenged-misogynoir)

expression have nothing to do with you, and it is unfair for you to comment on it, albeit from some moral higher ground. How can you look down on something you don't know enough about? Wow, Cardi B would have a field day with that one. Hell, Nicki Minaj would too, and she was starting to get famous around that time. Not that Ethan would notice.

Besides *Blazing Saddles* and his beliefs about rap music, I still enjoyed listening to music and watching movies and TV shows with Ethan and those other folks. And there was one show that solidified our friendship: a crime comedy with a Black and White buddy team. Ooh, I cannot tell you how excited I was to find out that Ethan and I both love this show! This show was relatively early in its run, so we could re-watch reruns and watch new episodes live. (Is that a thing that people do anymore? Watch shows when they air? Oh, I miss that. Part of it was for the fresh experience of watching something brand new, but also, if we missed it, we had to wait a little while to catch that episode again. It was the era of on-demand, but not instantaneous on-demand or DVR.)

In addition to Ethan and me, Jacq liked the show and would often watch the shows with us. Jacq was there the whole time, watching the movies and shows with us in the common room. I guess I was more vocal in my commentary than she was. That was a stark difference between the two of us. I had no problem trash-talking about any show that was on that I did not like. If I loved it, I said it; if I didn't, they heard it. I did also have very high standards for quality. I had a critique for every show I watched, even the ones I liked. I believe I got it from my family. You know the Prince song When Doves Cry lyrics: "*Maybe I'm just like my mother. She's never satisfied*"? Yup, that's me. We bonded over our piercing critiques of the media, believing that there was no such thing as the perfect movie or a great one. They could always do better. Wow, what a stereotypical Caribbean way of thinking.

So I brought that way of socializing into college, not realizing that some people dislike having those direct and blunt conversations. Even more, some people may find it aggressive or combative. What??? I had no idea. Being open and debating topics was how I tried to bond with people. How was I supposed to know I shouldn't have been so vocal and different? I can tell you who did know: Jacq.

Chapter Eight // Jacq and the Giant Disney Collection?

Ah, Jacq. The more I got to know her, the less I realized I knew about her. I could probably say the same thing today. How can I characterize someone who intrigued and frustrated me, who alienated and resonated with me at the same time? I don't want this to sound like the stereotypical catfight scenario: two women competing fiercely to win the hearts of their friends and their lovers. Because there honestly was no competition, at least from my end. I do not like competing with people for other people's affection, friends, or romantic interests. Consciously, the idea of competition turned me off. This was a pattern for me that predated high school. Once I saw that someone was trying to "win the crowd" or be the life of the party, I backed away. One reason was that I never thought I would win. At first glance, this may seem like an indicator of low self-esteem, but it was not. Why would I, a sushi roll, compete for the top prize in a cheeseburger-filled world? It's not that the sushi doesn't belong at the cafeteria; it just doesn't make sense for it to be around a competition created for and mainly the primary interest of cheeseburgers. It was the cheeseburger who wanted to have a competition when the sushi was just okay with chilling out with the other types of food.

Let's think of it another way, using real people. Imagine a scenario where people were hanging out and having a cool normal conversation. Then randomly, someone shouts, "Hey, who wants to do a bodybuilding contest," and starts lifting heavyweights in a high-paced manner. You'd be like, "Um, where did you get those weights?" and then you would be confused, right? But because we live in a health and beauty-obsessed world, people start to feel pressured to compete with one another or cheer the self-appointed participants onward. Soon enough, everyone joins in some sort of fashion, whether directly or indirectly. But no one ever thinks to

50

question the purpose of everything in the first place. I'd be the one who would look and say, "No, I don't want to do that," and either walk away or question the purpose of all of this out loud. And I wouldn't be doing it out of some grand, self-righteous gesture. I would respond that way because I clearly did not understand the game or its rules. But I would be the odd person out.

And that, folks, *is the core of the White female psyche*.

Haha, no. I'm kidding. Or am I? But I almost blew your mind with that revelation, right? I must have been alluding to some group of people. Maybe. The truth is that deep down, I was connected to Jacq. I will only say this once: I may have loved her. And feel free to take that in whatever way you want.

Once the social cliques settled and solidified, and I learned everyone's names, I started to bond more with Jacq over shared or intriguing interests. We both like similar movies, tv, and music. Jacq had a fierce Disney movie obsession. I learned from her that many young girls grew up watching all the Disney movies. She showed me her CD and DVD collection, which had all the major hits along with some other classic movies such as *Breakfast at Tiffany's*. I had seen a few Disney movies growing up, but I was never interested in collecting them.. I soon learned that many other girls besides Jacq grew up beaming in anticipation of the next film to add to their ongoing collection. The main issue I had with Disney movies was their tendency to be sappy romantics. I loved rom-coms, but the difference was that rom-coms were earthier and not as unrealistic and fantastical.

Jacq had a mission to expose the other women and me on the floor to her broad collection. I was interested enough to join in her quest. Looking back, I now realize that I had a pattern of watching movies, even ones I did not like, out of the sheer purpose of entertainment itself. I would complain if I didn't like it, but I would still watch. I guess it never occurred that I could walk away.

About thirteen movies in, we decided one night to watch the 2007 movie *Enchanted.* But us girls were not alone that night. Soon enough, some of the boys entered the common room and never left. They began to complain in a similar way I would. However, I wasn't complaining nearly as much during this movie. I maybe liked it? *Wait, what was happening to me?*

Ethan and Robert were among the group of men who stayed and complained. And at one point, one of the women said "If you don't like it, you know you can leave, right?" Silence. A brief but poignant silence swept the room. It got me thinking, *did they hear her?* Yup, they did. But, if you stay quiet long enough, you can make people question their reasoning, and then escape facing an uncomfortable truth. A tactic that White people do very well, I learned years later.

Enough fucking around. Anyway, the more movies I watched, the more I enjoyed movies I never thought I would. Then there was the moment that shattered my cold heart. During one scene of *Love Actually*, I made an audible "*Awww*" sound. And no, it wasn't the stupid cue-card stalker scene. It doesn't matter what made me do it. What mattered was how the room responded. There was shock followed by affirmative cheers and applause. "Yes, we finally cracked her!" Jacq snickered. "Nope," I said, with a sly smile. Fuck, she got me.

Another aspect of Jacq that I liked, or more specifically enjoyed, was her baking. Yes, in addition to her interest in Disney movies, she also had a great interest in baking all types of sweets. I was happy to see the joy on her face as she prepped and cooked, and my stomach was even happier to receive her baked goods. It was a treasure I never knew I wanted.

My mother was (um, still is) a great cook. When I was younger, I took for granted her skill in this, how she was able to bring Caribbean recipes that she learned as a child (yes, child) into our home. I used to be so picky and had such a little appetite (okay, I still am) that I never truly appreciated her food. Even worse, I often begged her to abandon her home meals and cook Americanized foods instead. She didn't like it at all, but she adapted and created meals from "America" to suit my tastes (re: popular in America, because guess what, many of our favorite foods in this country came from other countries).

Even with her amazing skills, there was one area in cooking in which she could not perfect, and that was baked goods. Well, sort of. She could not master making baked goods from scratch. Give her some prepped boxes, and the food still slaps, but I remember my mother saying that she always wanted to learn how to make those meals from scratch but could never quite get it right.

So by the time I came to college, I only knew of the world of baked goods by way of Betty Crocker and Duncan Himes. Good people. Until I met Jacq. Now, it wasn't just the fact that she enjoyed baking. I knew of other people throughout my life who could do the same. However, I was never invited into the baking process to the point that I became the regular recipient of her finished products. I never had someone who wanted to bake for me. It was a pleasant surprise. She also tried, more than once, to teach me how to bake, but I vehemently refused, stating that I would be a better recipient than helper. I was hesitant for a couple of reasons. First, I did not know how to cook. Or I guess I should say that I refused to learn how to cook. I still don't know how I developed such a strong opinion at a very young age, but I vividly remember making the decision before the age of ten that I would not learn to cook.

My mother was the housewife and the homemaker, which meant she was the only one who cooked for us. As children, that made perfect sense. We were too young to cook for ourselves. And it also made sense to me that she would make large meals like dinner for the entire family, which was not that large to begin with. However, I became annoyed, for some reason, that my mother would make my father his lunch every single day. Why it annoyed me so much, I have no real clue. I think it was because I began to notice that he would go without eating that meal if she did not make him lunch. And this happened long after I learned how to use the toaster at age seven and make my own school lunches at age ten. I felt like I was putting in the effort to learn at least that much in terms of food prep, but the man of the house did not have to. I was a very adultified child, very mature about my academics and other responsibilities. I began to compare myself to him, and I noticed the gender double standard very early in life. Perhaps it was so easy that it became an oversimplified one, yet that belief system permeated through my psyche at that time, leading into adolescence and young adulthood.

I soon equated cooking to femininity, and I did like how I saw too many examples in life and in the media of women carrying the load more often than men. I soon began to hold the strong belief that women learned to cook only for the sake of a man. Therefore, I opted out of learning at an early age. Let me just say that I regretted that decision many years later since my decision not to cook also included me not learning for myself, which as a single adult, was not a wise choice. Ugh. Unfortunately, I held low-key resentment towards my mother for always making my father his lunches. It wasn't until college and through Jacq that I started to feel guilty about my beliefs. Yup, a White woman opened my eyes to the complexities of the matter and how unfair I was being to my mother. But please, White women, don't grow a big head about this. Let's focus on Black here.

So, Jacq had designated me, as well as the other members of our squad, the royal tasters and consumers of her lovely cuisine that she made quite often. It became a regular addition to our movie nights. I finally learned that cooking was not only about assuming a feminine role, which, unfortunately, I had long equated to an inferior, passive role. Cooking can bring people together. More importantly, many people cook to communicate love, care, and joy to other people's lives. Jacq wasn't doing it to win people over; it was genuinely a way to show that she liked us and how she considered her important to her life, that she could share that side of herself. I felt honored to be a part of that, a part of her world.

It made me think of my mother. *How could I possibly understand the complexity of her situation?* I was siding with a very narrow trope of feminism where I decided every woman who chose to cook for a male partner was giving up her own power and only giving in to the demands of men. There are more nuances to that situation. I began to pay more attention to the dynamics of my parent's household responsibilities. I began to ask more deliberate questions about their roles in the household. My father took pride in his role as the breadwinner and being a father. Being a provider meant going to work so we could have the finances to meet our basic needs and luxuries. One of my mother's roles was to make the food so those needs could be met. And because my father was gone at work during the afternoon and evening, preparing food beforehand helped him out. Meal prepping, in general, helped the family survive, ensuring that we all always had something to eat. While I still, to this day, do not completely agree with the traditional gendered aspects of those roles, or the fact that it was not without its flaws, I did acknowledge that it was a system that worked for them. And quite frankly, it was none of my business to question everything as an outsider of sorts.

Yup, so Jacq made me learn to understand and appreciate my mother more for those aspects of our lives. I was also able to expand my understanding and open myself up to the possibilities of the many shades of femininity. I used to condemn traditional femininity due to its historical ties to submission to the patriarchy. But I began to realize that I could engage in those types of activities and not be weak or submissive for doing so. Because it was my choice, and an active one that I could participate in however I wanted to, to my accord. I still loved the masculine aspects of my self-expression, but I grew to embrace the complexities of gender expression, in general, and not limit myself to one side or the other.

So I became part of Jacq's regular studio audience, watching her in the common kitchen area as she made her signature sweets. "Go ahead, Rachael Ray!" I would exclaim to myself as she maneuvered around the space with finesse and ease. Granted, she wasn't doing anything extra special, but she had the ability to make the simple pleasures sparkle. Plus, she made them for me, putting a pep in my step. Out of all of her creations, it's the brownies for me.

Ah, yes. I remembered the first time I had her brownies. What a magical face palm moment. She just took them out of the oven and set them on the counter to cool.

"Yay, can't wait to eat them," I said as I headed away from the counter and towards the door.

"Well, you don't have to wait. C'mon, grab a piece!" Jacq said, smiling.

"Um, don't we have to wait a while before eating them?"

"*No*," she said, slightly confused.

"Well, I don't want to get diarrhea from eating them too soon…"

"WHAT?!" Jacq chuckled, almost choking on her bite. "Where did you hear that from?"

"My muh…muh...muh…" I stumbled and cut myself off, like the backup vocals in Lady's Gaga's Poker Face.

"That sounds like something parents tell their kids, so they don't skip dinner and go straight to dessert."

"Huh? Wait, no…" I couldn't believe it.

Have my parents been lying to me this WHOLE time?

"Haha, never mind." I nervously shook off the embarrassment. I cautiously walked over and took a piece. I

56

stared at it for a second, blew on it, and then ate it. "Yum, this tastes good!"

"Yeah, it does. You're so weird, Pia." She smirked, and then we both started cracking up.

"I know." I don't know who needs to hear this, but I did not end up getting diarrhea that day or any time afterward. Old wives' tales die hard.

After spending some more time with Jacq, I got a better sense of her tastes in movies and TV. You know, when you share certain things in common, like background and upbringing, you can guess what things people are into and what they would not? Oh, this is based on stereotypes, but also it could be an educated guess based on patterns. For example, if you gave a list of movies you liked, and they all seemed to be in the genre of horror films, would you be surprised if a person got excited about a children's film? Yes, *right*?

I say this because the more group conversations I had with Jacq in the mix, the more I slowly noticed discrepancies in her interests. Some of you may think I am biased and only relying on "stereotypical interests" to base my opinion, and maybe you are right. I learned over time that folks can have complex and varied interests and tastes. However, this was not what was happening here. Maybe it's this: I was better at spotting her lies than I realized.

Over time, our groups shifted from the all-girls Disney group to the more regular mixed group that consisted of Jacq, me, Ethan, and Robert. So I was learning more about Ethan and Robert's interests at the same time I was growing in my knowledge of Jacq. I slowly started noticing discrepancies in what she said, especially around Ethan. And the crazy part, I knew right away when she was lying, and I rarely questioned

57

myself. I have always second-guessed my thoughts across so many different situations, so I surprised myself with my confidence in my bullshit detector.

The first clear example was also in the realm of TV shows. We were discussing our favorite shows, and Ethan mentioned *Battlestar Galactica*. Now, I have never seen that show, but I heard of it and know that it was sci-fi. So I was a bit surprised when Jacq exclaimed, "Me too! I love that show." Really? She liked that show. How come it's the first time I heard about this? Once again, I understand that she could have had an interest in sci-fi that I did not know of, and this could have been one of her favorite shows. That's not it. Then I realized it wasn't what she said but how she said it. Up until now, Jacq was not a very animated person. Maybe that was one of the parts I liked about her. She was girly and feminine but not extra about it. But when it came to conversations like these, she became much more vivacious. Not overly so, but enough that I noticed a change to make me question her genuineness in those situations. I just knew it. I just knew that she did not like that show or did not find it nearly as interesting as she was making it to be. So why would she lie about it to him?

In college, I had to learn a hard lesson about the art of conversation and, more importantly, talking... It took me years to fully absorb this, but I did not know that some people would lie or exaggerate just to bond and form a connection with others. I knew to the extent that people who got along and were friends tended to like similar things, but I did not know that some people would change themselves or appear to make it look like they had way more in common with their peers than they did. I was under the impression that you could bond with people based on differences in addition to similarities. So I thought I could openly not like certain things my friends enjoyed and still build a close bond with them. But apparently, that's not the case?

But Jacq knew this. She knew this very well. And slowly, I became the side non-player character in the weird real-life game Trivial Pursuit because clearly, this pursuit was nonsensical and beyond trivial to me. For a long time, I didn't even know there was a game, playing right in front of me.

Turns out that I am not the only person who did not understand the rules of the game. But during this time in college, I was. You ever read an academic article several years later about communication differences across cultures and was like: "Shit, That me! There is a secret social language I was unaware of!"

Time to bring out the citations, y'all. Some people were raised to create bonds by blending into the group, frequently to the point of changing their interests and hobbies to fit into the group. Some folks were raised to believe that they are to keep the harmony, even when they disagree or have different opinions because the goal is to maintain the bond and relationship at all costs (mostly). And other people were raised to seek truth and speak openly and honestly, even if it is to the point that there is disagreement within the group. Other people were raised to believe the goal is bond and connection, but it takes a backseat to truth and sincerity. I was today years old when I learned that some of my past and current colleagues were raised to stay silent and muffle their feelings out of the concern that it would disrupt group harmony. They didn't believe in stifling strongly-held beliefs or non-negotiables, but they were more lenient with leaving some less important differences and disagreements unsaid. Other people were raised to believe that truth, no matter how disruptive or uncomfortable it may seem, should always be spoken, with the belief that the group could handle the discord and move forward closer than ever by working through conflict. Fascinating as fuck, isn't it?

I hope you can tell me which group I belong to. At some level, I can't fault some people. The goal is to create long-lasting relationships based on harmony and minimal open conflict. Ideally, that would be a great relationship, so it wouldn't hurt to make some white lies, right? Who cares if some people lie or exaggerate certain interests in things if they just want to connect and build friendships and romantic relationships? If it doesn't hurt that person, then it should work, right?[4]

If you think I am going to justify some people's behaviors solely "just cause," then you are sorely mistaken. I'm empathetic, but to a certain point. Yes, I can't fault some people for engaging in those behaviors if it only affects them. But oftentimes, it doesn't just affect them. It affects the people who are part of the larger group around them. And it most definitely clashes with other people's communication styles and beliefs. And that, folks, was the start of the downfall of the first domino.

After the *Battlestar Galactica* fiasco, I started to identify other discrepancies in Jacq's thoughts, interests, and behaviors. One notable example is rap music. *Memba that*? We all know how Ethan feels about that. But when it came to Jacq, I thought it was something we both liked. And that was true, as evidenced by her iPod playlist. However, she never shared that playlist with Ethan and never joined me in complaining about his deeply held beliefs...

I am not saying I am a noble person who preaches to others, "Thou shall not lie!" People lie all the time, and so do I. Sometimes I find it fun and entertaining to lie, to get away with something, or manipulate situations in my favor. Please,

---

[4] Citations, as promised: "White Female Culture" (conspireforchange.org/white-female-culture)
"The Truth About Our Differences" (blackenterprise.com/the-truth-about-our-differences)
"Taking back the power: an analysis of Black women's communicative resistance" (tandfonline.com/doi/abs/10.1080/15358593.2018.1461234)
"White Women Doing White Supremacy in Nonprofit Culture" (tzedeksocialjusticefund.org/white-women-doing-white-supremacy-in-nonprofit-culture)
"Some Aspects and Assumptions of White Culture in the United States" (cascadia.edu/discover/about/diversity/documents/Some%20Aspects%20and%20Assumptions%20of%20White%20Culture%20in%20the%20United%20States.pdf)

I'm not the only one who does this. At least I own it. What confused me were the types of situations I noticed Jacq lying about. It didn't make sense to me to lie or fake interest in other people's interests. It's not a moral thing for me. It's a sustainability thing. How can people keep that up for an extended period and remember all those lies in order? I could not see the benefit of it. A friendship or relationship, for what? Seems like too much work for something I wasn't interested in.

Also, I never thought lying was an option in those situations. I didn't realize people could tell lies about certain parts of their identity, which is what I believed hobbies and interests to be. They are a central part of who they are, shaping people into who they are. Maybe it comes from my parents. I was almost today-years-old when I learned that some parents would lie to their children growing up just to protect their children's feelings. Did other people know about this? I sure as hell did not. Once again, I understand that everyone has the innate ability to do this, but I thought it was against the parenting rules... You know, parents are supposed to feed you, bathe you, and shelter you, but not from the reality of the world. Lying to protect someone's feelings was just not an option that I was aware of, especially if the truth was too imperative. Especially if it is to prepare for the harsh realities of this often cruel world.

Despite Jacq's lying on certain interests, there was one show that all three of us desperately loved. It was a Black and White crime comedy that premiered right before college. And by Black and White, I mean literally, a Black Jamaican and White Hispanic buddy team that solved crimes under the guise of one of them being psychic. It was one of my favorite new shows to watch, and I was ecstatic to learn that. Finally, there was a show we could all agree to like from the start. This was the first time we also started binge-watching episodes late into the night together. Or at least it started that way.

By this point, I was getting used to talking late into the night, especially when we watched shows and played games together. I slowly was able to open up more about myself to others, and I was pleasantly surprised to find that they were accepting of it. It was a weird feeling for me to experience: having people genuinely wanting to spend time with me. Now we had a routine: do homework together, go to dinner together, and spend the weekend talking until the early hours of the morning. And I was looking forward to it. I had a squad. A squad of nerds, but still, wow.

Oh yeah, I forgot to mention another sign of my growing comfort with my new friend group: the couch. Before college, I had a massive personal bubble. No one could tell it was massive because it would only be an issue in social hangs, and as you could probably guess, I did not hang out with people outside of school that much. Nope, I was not a party animal. Though I could dance my ass off at school functions. Anyway, college was the first time I got to hang out with people outside the classroom, which was mostly in the common rooms. Now, this may seem like a minute detail, but I had never been in a regular social situation where I would need to lounge with folks in couches and chairs. It seems simple, right? Spending time with friends, chatting it up on couches. But for some reason, that scenario made me VERY uncomfortable. I didn't realize it until college when I would sit down on an oversized couch, and someone would sit RIGHT next to me. I thought a four-seater was a two-seater, but I was proven wrong. Maybe it's an East Coast thing. You see, especially in public transit, no one would sit directly next to someone else unless they knew them. So, it was really hard for me to casually sit closer to a group of people on the same couch.

I do not think other people realized my discomfort. Or maybe they did, and they chose not to say anything. Maybe uncomfortable is an understatement. I would feel sheer panic inside: my heart would race, my breathing would get shallow, and my legs would start twitching. I tried my best to hide my emotion because I knew I would look weird if I completely freaked out whenever someone wanted to sit near me. I was also surprised that I felt panic. This is not a skill I thought I had to learn in college: how to sit near people to converse with them.

Yes, even I knew back then that my panic was a trauma response, a trust issue with being near people. And then it dawned on me: how could I have spent so long in my life not being next to people and not even realizing it? I sat next to my peers at the classroom tables and desks in high school with no problem, but a simple couch in a large common room was a huge obstacle? Fuck. This was going to be a huge hill to climb.

It did help that we were doing things I enjoyed while on the couch. I wasn't taking a difficult exam or gazing into someone's eyes for a long time to build trust (it's a real thing: look it up)*. I found out that the more time I spent with them, getting to know them and sharing more of myself, the easier it was to sit next to them. I started to enjoy it. Feelings, amirite?

Why do I share this deep dark secret of mine? Well, after I got more used to the routine of hanging out with my squad, I slowly began to sense a bit of competition for couch time and binge time. It was mainly between, you guessed it, Jacq and me.

"Jacq and I, sitting in a tree (couch), K-I-S-S-I-N-G..."

Nope, not this time. Not a fan of the queerbaiting plot device here. Although, I sometimes think if we had just gotten along that well, it would have solved all our future problems.

I did not realize it then, but Jacq had her agenda. While I was trying to bond with the group, she was trying to bond with the group, and um, one person in particular.

Chapter Nine // The Pick Me Dilemma

I need to take an important deep dive into the psyche of a young woman here. As I mentioned before, my family and I did not realize that there were many different parts of college outside of academics. And while I started to get more used to the social part of college, I was unaware of a whole other aspect of that life.

I can't speak on behalf of African American young adult women or other Black (voluntary) immigrant women and their families, but I do know in my second-gen Black immigrant family, the goal of college was to get an education to land a career. That's it. This is a common goal for almost everyone who attends college, but there are also other goals: social ones. Many people go to college to find long-lasting friendships and romantic partners. I thought friendship was more of a byproduct than a goal, meaning if I bonded with folks and made deep connections with them, that was great, but I was not thinking of it as a goal in addition to getting good grades. And then there's the romance part of it. An aspect that was way more complicated than I realized.

Remember when I said I wanted to avoid romantic relationships out of fear of losing my scholarship? That was a real concern of mine. However, it was an easy boundary to place on myself because I did not have any real interest in finding a relationship, or a long-term one I should say. And, this is important, I thought I was part of a new generation of people who were not looking to find a marriage partner in college. Seriously. I honestly thought it was a matter of the past: a behavioral pattern I only saw in movies from an older era. Turns out the MRS degree was still a very active goal among folks in our college years, particularly women. It never dawned on me that there was a timeline for getting both an educational degree and finding a life partner within four years.

Maybe life partner is too restrictive of a word. I learned much later that people went into college intending to find a long-term relationship, not necessarily marriage, by the end of college, but it was a goal down the line. Once again, I thought a relationship, if anything, was maybe a byproduct of education, not a goal. Silly me. I also didn't have the desire to actively search for a long-term partner. I didn't think I could to become so infatuated with someone romantically and sexually to the point of locking things down for marriage. I was fucking still in my late teens, for goodness sake. Maybe it was trauma or lack of desire that caused a disconnect for me; I don't know. What I did know was that I did not believe in the concept of marriage.

Here's the thing: I did not want to become someone's wife. I had a real problem with that role in itself. Every time I think about this, I can imagine someone saying:

"But you can redefine your relationship for whatever works for you and your partner. You can get married and not subscribe to the traditional, oppressive definition of a wife if that's what you're thinking, Pia."

True, true. In perfect theory, it makes sense and can be done. But my problem wasn't with the internal aspects of marriage, but the societal views and behaviors toward married couples. I firmly believed that regardless of the redefined or egalitarian roles placed within that marriage, the wife will always continue to be oppressed. Whether you agree with me or not, being a "wife" was a no-no for me. The only way I could be liberated from that construct was to not partake in it in the first place.

Wasn't this chapter supposed to be about Jacq? Ah, yes, you're right. You see, Jacq did not come from a first/second gen immigrant family like me. She had other people in her family who went through college, and they were able to teach her about those little-known but very explicitly implicit rules of social life and dating. She also came from an upper-middle-class background, which means nothing in today's standards of socioeconomic class because the economy is trash and oppressively capitalist. (Whoops, sorry, my social justice side came out for a split second. She stays ready in the backstage wings, y'all.) Anyway, that meant that she was probably guaranteed certain things in life: paid education, access to jobs, housing, and other future assets for marriage. Why does all of this matter? Well, it means that she knew the rules and outcomes of the game of college life, y'all, and how education and marriage prospects were tied. I don't mean to say that she actively came to college looking for a ring. I don't even think she's that basic. But based on her actions, she looked like she had a five-year plan that may or may not include a man (It did.)[5]

What once were communal activities turned into opportunities for Jacq to close in on her target: Ethan. Oh, and let's not suggest that he was a passive member of this quest. Gosh, I hate to imply that: a man unknowingly falling prey to a crafty woman's charms. Bitch, please. He had to have known what was happening here. I think that is what worked well for them in this scenario. You have probably gotten the sense that Ethan is not a Casanova. It's not an insult at all. That's one of the things I liked about him. There was no hidden sexual or romantic agenda with him. He treated other women and me like any other peer he tried to get to know in college. And I'm not saying he should get an award for that, either. That's common decency 101. Basic human respect. He was able to follow that rule. So, because he was not the type to make the first move, it became easy for Jacq to pursue him as hard as she did.

Maybe she wasn't going that hard. She wasn't super aggressive. I think I considered it hard because I knew it was not genuine. At least when it came to the things she did. I could tell she would agree with Ethan to get along with him and impress him. That irked me. I don't think it's fair for someone to do that. I would not want someone to agree with

---

[5] "Through The Lens of Race: Black and White Women's Perceptions of Womanhood" (ncbi.nlm.nih.gov/pmc/articles/PMC5679014/)

me just to impress me. She also knew the subtle art of touch. That irked me as well. As I mentioned before, being in a close physical space was hard for me, and that discomfort also applied to touch. I never thought it was polite or comfortable to just touch someone. And I mean even the basic stuff: like a pat on the back or shoulder, a hug, anything beyond the introductory handshake. So it bothered the hell out of me that she would trick Ethan into holding hands with her. One time she did it by comparing hand sizes: "Oh look, your hand is twice the size of mine. See?" as she touched his palm with hers, out of the player's handbook.

I was getting better with physical proximity, but the touch part was still difficult, so it bothered me that Jacq could cross that line easily. I just wanted to be comfortable with touching people, period: to be able to rub a friend's shoulder to comfort them, to lightly slap someone's knee when they made me laugh. Subtle but genuine connection. So I became resentful that Jacq was being manipulative with her actions. But then again, don't hate the player, I guess? Hate the game. Can I get mad at both?

The things that she was doing, I found out years later, were very common flirting techniques. Stuff that they teach anybody and everybody to find a mate. So can I fault her for using the skills that everyone uses when trying to find a partner? Still, it did bother me that there was a lack of genuineness. It seemed canned, like a dating competition that I could see miles away. But wait, how can it be a competition when only one person is playing?[6]

What upset me the most was that her tactics directly impacted me. Being a "pick-me" (a term I also learned years later) turns any other person who could be competitive into a threat that must be eliminated. The thing is, well, there are many things. First, we played different games: I was playing

[6] "Are You Compromised or Compromising: The Danger of Living Life as a Pick Me!" (donnaoriowo.com/blog/are-you-compromised-or-compromising-the-danger-of-living-life-as-a-pick-me)

the friend game and she the dating game. Second, the idea of eliminating a perceived competitor was way too extreme. And Jacq did not do anything malicious. There were those negative comments about me that I later learned were passive-aggressive behavior. (More on that later). Most people would consider most of her behavior to be normal. She would slowly find ways to spend more alone time with him, even if it meant engaging in shared group interests with just the two of them. That meant binging shows and doing other activities that I liked, but only the two of them. Even the idea of spending more time with him, one on one, was isolating to me. It was hard to find time to bond when her needs superseded mine. Now I know what you are probably thinking: most people expect couples to spend more time with one another compared to their friends. That's how dating works: once you find your partner, you prioritize spending time with them over your other friends. The problem was that I did not know this was happening. I did not know how to develop friendships, let alone understand the hidden rules of courtship. There was a connection and bond that Ethan and I had, something I could not put a finger on. We were getting closer and enjoying our time. And all I saw was her taking him away from me. I wanted to spend more nights talking to him. I wanted to share the excitement of watching a new episode of a beloved show. Was I wrong to desire that too?

Apparently, this is a real issue that occurs within the dating realm. Some women are socialized to believe they must obtain a lover at any cost, even if it means disparaging other women and themselves in the process. The Pick-Me Girl, as it is aptly called. Ugh, why wasn't TikTok around when I needed it? It would have been super simple just to share a video and say, "See? This is you boo!" Well, in terms of late-00s technology, we could only mainly rely on books and hearsay.[7]

---

[7] "The Problem With TikTok's "Pick-Me Girl" Trend Is More Complicated Than You Think" (insidehook.com/article/internet/pick-me-girl-tiktok-trend-explained)

I would not classify Jacq to be the outright stereotypical Pick-Me. The most common examples you hear are the ones where women would go out of their way to show their love interests the many ways they are different from a normal woman. That they understand men and are a better companion based on their shared values and interests, which are not typical female interests. The topper of the trope is that these Pick-Me will openly criticize other women just to get into their crush's good graces. Women hating on women; you get the gist. Jacq was not like that. Her ways were much more subtle to recognize; there, I say it, it fell within the normal range. Or common range, because this shit was not normal or cool. That was perhaps the most frustrating aspect of this whole ordeal. There I was, clearly seeing the disingenuousness within Jacq's attempts to connect with Ethan.[8]

However, what she was doing was par for the course regarding dating and courtship. Aren't we taught to find things in common with someone to gain their interest? And if it wasn't a complete match, what's the harm in embellishing some details, right? It's not an outright lie if you didn't necessarily like the show your bae likes, but you've technically seen it, right? It's not like no one has ever lied before when it comes to meeting and getting to know people; even I am not above that, and I never thought I was.

Enough complimenting this White woman. I want to get into my feelings. Shit, now I feel guilty for saying that. Slightly. How can I explain what I felt as while these events unfold? It was like watching a train crash in slow motion. Or a dumpster fire that no one acknowledged existing in front of our very eyes. The cruel nature of this conquest was that it could not coexist with my quest for male friendship. That's the fucked up part of all of this. When it comes to friendship and dating, dating is a far superior relationship. No matter what stage of life, society places more meaning on dating than on

---

[8] "10 Signs You're a "PICK ME" Woman" (curlynikki.com/2018/08/10-signs-youre-pick-me-woman.html)

friendships. We even have sayings such as "I married my best friend." Why do we do that? Why is the ultimate friend the one you have to marry? Isn't there room for both?

I didn't have the chance to explore my thoughts and feelings about friendships in college before the opportunity started to get away from me. I knew I was probably getting into tricky, uncharted territory because I was trying to make friends with men. However, I felt like it was just another viable option like other genders. All I knew was that I liked spending time with these people. And the more time I spent with Ethan, the more I liked spending time with him. It was that simple for me.

At that time in my life, it was hard for me to become interested in people again. To like them consistently and more rarely to become more intrigued by them the more time I spent with them. By the time I finished high school, there was no spark. Or I should say, there was no sustainable spark with anyone. Now, I could socialize with existing peers, meet new people, and have a relatively pleasant time, but there was a disconnect. There were just people I knew I could have a good time with, but nothing would develop into a continued friendship.

In my senior year, it became evident how I viewed interpersonal relationships and excitement when completing a classroom exercise in my English class. One of our classmates, guest-teaching the class one day, asked us to define happiness. I remember defining it in terms of something temporary and fleeting. Sure, I could experience brief moments of positive emotions, but the state of happiness was not a real or obtainable concept. I was not the only one who felt that way, but my peer teacher was quite horrified by my morbid definition. But I stood firm in my beliefs. At that time, I had not experienced prolonged periods of happiness to consider it a true emotional state. Years later, I was able to identify that thought pattern. What was it called? Oh yeah, it was depression.

Back to the couch. The couch became a space where I could slowly reconnect with my feelings and physical state and start to feel more consistent states of happiness. I started to change the meaning of life from being mostly sad with brief positive feelings to mostly positive feelings with some moments of sadness that I could cope with.

What was more significant in redefining happiness was that I realized that real happiness wasn't bursts of sheer excitement but feelings of simple calmness and peace. And Ethan became a major part of that transition for me. Ugh, I'm not trying to base my happiness solely on a man. He was a part of a larger picture. It was him within the larger context of college life: academics, social events, friends, talking, and doing homework. Really simple, boring things that I found happiness and comfort in. And it gave me hope to find that happiness within and beyond that context.

Maybe that's why I liked spending time with Ethan. He was someone whose presence comforted me and gave me peace. He wasn't special. And I don't mean it disrespectfully. He wasn't extravagant or flashy or any of those other things that society told me I should find intriguing in a partner or a friend. Like the dangerous bad guy or member of a rambunctious crew. Or the super-sculpted vain model or the group of ultra-pretty friends obsessed with their pretty looks. And I don't mean that he was ugly. I guess his face was symmetrical or something like that. I wasn't paying attention. What I mean is that I'm not into that extra stuff. His simplicity was what made him special, at least to me. Oh, and Jacq. I guess she found that special too.

This made for a very unbalanced situation. A hierarchical situation where one person's needs were more legitimate than another's. Why did one have to be more important? It became a seesaw of entangled interactions since we still spent time as a group. Slowly, I started to notice them pair off. We would all stay up all night until the early hours of the morning, and when the rest of us went to sleep, they stayed behind. That part did not necessarily bother me. I wasn't going to stay awake indefinitely for anyone's attention. What irked me was consistently sneaking away to engage in hobbies that we all found enjoyable. The buddy-psychic cop show we once watched as a group every week became something shared between the two of them. And yes, this was before binging, and on-demand episodes were standard, so you can imagine how annoyed I was to have to wait for the reruns to air. What are reruns, Gen-Zers? Ain't nobody got time to explain that. Google it if you haven't already. See? I get so cranky when I'm not caught up on shows that it hurts to think about past examples.

Why did this bother me so much? I would often ask myself at the time. It took me so long to get comfortable spending time with people regularly that I got annoyed when it looked like it would end. OR I should say, I got annoyed when I thought someone was unfairly manipulating the situation to their benefit. Look, I would have been perfectly fine with boundaries. Once again, I am not a fan of spending a hundred percent of your time together just for the sake of things. I like space and freedom. There was something about Jacq's courting ways that seemed eerily malcontent. I admit that there was some enmeshment at times. However, I wished things were more explicit: Were we all a group hanging, a group and a couple hanging, or were they just a couple hanging alone? I was so confused.

The most confusing aspect of the whole ordeal was that I never knew when they started dating. They never announced it to the group as a whole. You know, the folks that hung out with them 90 percent of the time? A brief announcement in the common room, a group text, a phone call, an email. Any form of communication would suffice. That was perhaps the most bitter aspect of all. I never heard from them that they were dating. How was that possible? Were they ashamed to tell me? Did they think it was obvious? They weren't kissing or fucking around me, so no, it wasn't obvious. The only faint clue was briefly mentioned during dinner one night.

Jacq calmly said at the table, "So, there's been this guy I went to high school with who started stalking me on FB. Asking me all these questions about me in college and if I was seeing someone. So I changed my FB profile status to 'in a relationship' to get him to back off. So, if you noticed that change, that's why."

"Okay…?" I said slowly, confused about the whole scenario and why she was mentioning this now.

Jacq just gave a sheepish smile. Robert became a bit intrigued and looked as if he was going to ask follow-up questions, but he didn't. He just repeated what she said for clarification and then dropped it like the rest of us. *Was that the big announcement? Really, Jacq? You're going to make something simple so complicated?* No, no, no.

Do you know how I eventually found out? It was from the only Black dude on the floor who randomly walked into the common room one day and congratulated the new couple…

"Sorry I was out of the loop for the past month. Great to hear you're finally together!"

What the FUCK? I was the main Black person they hung out with and the motherfucking only other Black dude on the floor, who lived waaay on the other side and saw us very rarely, had the scoop on me. I was the designated Black representative of this squad, and I should have been the first one with the tea! Okay, hunny?

I promise I'm not the jealous type, but something doesn't add up. Weird, right? That's the thing about Jacq. The more I knew her, the less I knew who she was and what she was truly thinking. I have to admit:that mysterious air about her attracted me. Like, you think you got someone all figured out, but there's a hidden part that's not completely revealed. And I admired someone who did not put all their cards on the table. Someone who believed you only got a taste of them, not everything at once, and you had to work to get to know the

73

other parts of them. Was this her personality, or was it just all part of a bigger plan of hers?

Now that I had found out the big secret, I started looking back and cringed at all the missed cues. I suddenly thought of the one time we walked back from campus at night to our dorm. We laughed over some silly shit as we crossed the under bridge, and I got the rare desire to poke Ethan in the side due to something funny he said. I positioned myself behind him and leaned on the opposite side for the poke, getting ready to shout surprise after he tried to figure out who did it. But as I did it, Jacq miraculously appeared beside him, and he leaned over to ask: "Hey… Did you do that?

"Nope, I didn't," Jacq said with a coy smile.

Ethan shook his head. "Yeah, you did."

"No, it wasn't me."

Ethan smiled and shook his head lightly in disbelief. She grinned as we continued to walk back home.

Ugh, cringe! Was that flirting? How did I miss that? It was so subtle and fast, but I remember feeling disappointed and rejected for him not noticing me. I also felt cheated. Why couldn't I get the chance to express playful affection toward a friend of mine? Maybe it's because I rarely do it; when I do, I remember it vividly, and it is more memorable if I get rejected. Then again, I was upset that Jacq did not clarify it was me. At the time, I thought she may not have known it was me, but who else would it be? Robert's tall, skinny ass? Sure, men can poke and fool around with each other, but I've never seen him do it that way.

Every time she did subtle things like that, it became a game of give-and-take. When we should have all gotten to know each other as a group, she was carving her way to Ethan, and I was doing the same, but for different reasons. Unfortunately, we didn't get a chance to carve a path toward each other simultaneously. Yet, I still felt that Jacq was often invested in me. After all, we liked the same things and the same people, so shouldn't we get along? She was an attentive and good listener, and I was able to open up to her in similar ways to Ethan. How do you know if a woman friend truly likes you? Somehow, I felt she did like me deep down. She just had different priorities in terms of who she was closest aligned with, I guess.

I don't want to make excuses for messed-up behavior. But I often wonder about the aspects of this whole courtship situation that made it so bothersome to me, especially when many other people would regard it as acceptable and predictable behavior in the dating game. I guess the question is: should one go through lengths to prioritize their romantic needs over someone else's friendship needs? Or are my ambiguous needs for friendship worth casting away for *love*?

Chapter Ten // The First and Last Time I Ordered from the Applebee's Diet Menu

Back when I had borderline eating issues early in college, I spent my days exploring the glorious diet menus of many fast-food restaurants. It was a strange and curious time for me.

So, *one time at Applebee's...*

Wait, did I just minimize a potentially serious issue out of discomfort? Maybe. It was a fucked up time in my life, but it was just a moment, so I won't bore you with the details. For the sake of exposition, let's move on!

Okay, maybe that was a bit abrupt. It was just a weird moment in time for me. I was either underweight or thin almost my entire life: the tiny, short person with a spunky attitude. College was the first time I gained a significant amount of weight, and honestly, it wasn't that much: 15 pounds. Enough to transition from underweight to normal, whatever the hell that meant. But it was enough of a change to concern me back then: was I getting too fat? I didn't like talking about my weight since it can be a contentious topic. And most times, I felt like people would not take me seriously since I was still skinny.

At a certain point that first year, I got so stressed about balancing life and academics that I instinctively turned to something I could control: my food choices. But I had a horrible time defining what was healthy for me. I distinctly remember my friends making fun of what I thought were healthy foods. So I got quiet and focused inward. No more consulting other people. Perhaps that was a blessing in disguise.

I am very fortunate that the time I spent being hyper-focused on my food choices was short, but it could have easily gone down a slippery slope. I generally did not have a large appetite, so letting go of even more choices irritated me. Still, I decided to explore my options for the sake of, dare I say it, conformity. And that included dining out. I do look fondly back at those times in college when I frequently hung out with friends at food joints. And maybe it's just me, but why do it be always going down at Applebee's? I remember us being all souped-up just to head to a place that wasn't technically 5 stars in service, but us youngsters always had a 5-star experience.

That night was not one of those times. At least for me. We sat down at the table as the waiter handed the six of us our menus. I quickly turned to the diet menu and started perusing the choice list. There were few favorable options, and I questioned myself about sticking to this diet.

As I finally settled on my choice of what appeared to be a dry piece of white chicken and basic potatoes, Jacq positioned herself spine-high and gave a coy smile to the group.

"So, I had an interesting dream last night."

"Oh," somebody at the table said. I honestly don't remember, y'all. Time fades memories, especially meaningless minor details like this. "What was it about?" they probably asked.

"Well, I got back to our suite and was getting ready for bed. When I walked into my room, I saw Pia and Ethan naked in my bed," Jacq ended her short tale casually. Then the table fell silent.

Naked in bed. Okay. That's odd and random, I thought to myself. *Why would we just be chillin' on the bed like that?* A few seconds passed before I understood. Oh, she meant in bed, DOING STUFF! At that moment, I had two questions burning inside of me: "Did I look like I was enjoying myself, and did I cum?" I felt detached and curious, like a child looking through a Christmas store window, fascinated by the toys inside. Then I started to feel a knot in my stomach, slowly getting tighter as I became annoyed.

I must admit a dark secret to you, my dear readers. I was immediately curious because Jacq described a dream scenario I had never been able to experience myself. I have never been able to fantasize about sex in my waking state, and I rarely experience sex dreams. Adolescence and young adulthood are typically the prime time for people to have top-shelf sex fantasies, but I have always struggled to have them. And believe me, I've tried. I have spent nights lying in bed, trying to picture myself engaging in some sort of sexual activity, whether it was kissing or intercourse, but I could never get myself there. Let me clarify: this was not an issue of shame. I was not embarrassed to think about sex. I just could not physically produce the images of engaging in sex in my mind. I could picture myself, I could picture my sex object, but I could not picture the two (or more) of us together engaging in physical or sexual intimacy. And I did not receive pleasure from that, but I did not receive disgust either. Only numbness or frustration. The closest concept I believe it is similar to is the phenomenon where people are unable to produce images of objects in their heads. If you tell them to think of the word, "apple," they would not be able to see a picture of it, only the word. Google that shit; it's a real thing. My situation is almost similar to that, but my mind can produce some fragmented images.

I have been deeply ashamed of this. I used to think it was internalized guilt from societal and religious influences. And while I think that is true to an extent, I began to realize during high school that it was more of a sexual and emotional visual disconnect. I had plenty of celebrity crushes back then, but I struggled to actually think about having sex with them. For a long time, I thought it was normal to have a crush but not fantasize about them. Then I compared my experiences with others, and they did not match up. Could I truly say that I had sexual feelings for those crushes when I could not imagine having sex with them? The only rare times I was able to do this was in spontaneous dreaming states, but it was always with someone I knew in real life. For some weird reason, that was the requirement for me. It had to be with someone I knew or was connected to in real life. And that rarely happened.

So back to this knucklehead Jacq at the Applebee's. There I was, never able to have a sex dream, and there she goes flaunting it in my face! She has the dude and literally the fantasy. The audacity of whiteness, y'all. Can you believe it? It was another full two seconds later when I realized that maybe she might have suspected something was going on with us, like an affair.

NAW, that can't be it! No one has ever seen me as romantic competition, let alone someone who could steal a man. I quickly and awkwardly laughed it off. But then I felt guilty like I had done something wrong. So I sat in silence. And if you're wondering how Ethan took it, his response didn't help. "OH YEAH!" he said in a slow deep voice as if to suggest he enjoyed the idea of being in bed with me.

Looking back, I have to admit that response was hilarious. It was something only a White man can do without getting any verbally negative response from his White woman partner (stereotypically speaking). Let a Black man do that around his Black partner; his ass would have been cussed out. By the both of us, most likely. Fucked up, I know. Oh, and remember the other people at the table? They sat in silence as well. White people being silent during tense situations: will be a running theme in my life.

As we were all walking back to the car after dinner, Jacq casually said, "Oh, actually, when I got closer, it turned out to be Ethan and Robert in the bed." That's it. Then she just popped herself in the car. The rest of us gave puzzled looks at each other as we piled into the car ourselves. I mean, maybe she was right. We did share a little resemblance.

79

Robert, with his six-foot pale White ass, and my short-ass five-foot self. Spitting images.

Chapter Eleven // From Seeing Grey to Color: The First Spark

During the first semester of college, I was still meeting and seeing new people around campus. I had my days pleasantly occupied contently with academics and my friend group. I did not feel that I needed anything else. As we were hanging out for our usual dinner, I noticed Robert sneaking away occasionally to talk on his phone in a hushed tone. When we got closer, we realized he would do a baby voice when speaking to a particular person on the phone. It turned out it was his long-term girlfriend from high school. Wow, I got to pay better attention to detail. I'm pretty sure he probably mentioned her before. But to see the love magic in person was another story. So I learned that he had been dating his girlfriend from high school, who was still a senior... As I spent more nights with him, we got used to his routine of sneaking off at night to say goodnight to his partner. Ah, how sweet. It was alright, I guess. Not my taste, but to each their own.

I spent so much time with my squad that I did not think of anything as I paraded around with them on campus as if having a security team of tall White men. Robert, Ethan, Jacq, and I would have dinner together, and to the naked eye, it appeared as if we were double dating. But obviously, that was not true since Robert and Ethan had girlfriends. Yes, I was the only single person in our group of four, and I fucking loved it! Okay, maybe I didn't have that intense of a reaction, but it didn't bother me as much. Once again, friendships were the goal for me. That is, until one fine brunch-filled day.

What time is the perfect time for brunch, anyway? Do you go early morning, mid-morning, or later? I was never a morning person, so I enjoyed a much later brunch. Fuck it, you could call it lunch. Well, I liked to sleep on the weekends, so if I decided to go to brunch, it would be alone or with my squad much closer to the early afternoon... Do you remember those times? Waking up after 12 and thinking it was early? How did I do that? How could I wake up so late in the day and not die of hunger pangs?

Every once in a while, about once a month, we had floor brunches where everyone would head over as a group at the same time together. And doggone it, the RAs dared to make us head over to the cafeteria bright and early at 11:30 AM. The things I do for peer bonding. I should get a medal for participation. I had gone to a few of them before, and after a while, I did not feel as miserable getting up earlier in the day to attend. One fine Saturday morning-ish, Ethan and I headed over with the group of our floormates. We got our regular large group of tables in the middle of the cafeteria, and this time I sat across and slightly diagonal from him.

We grabbed our plates and filled them with the usual stuff. For me, cheese omelets are the sweet spot. Everything that day was typical; there was nothing out of the ordinary. People were having a good time, chatting about all sorts of things. As usual, I would sit back and listen and occasionally chimed in. Ethan was the same: he was the quiet one who hung back but would speak up once in a while if something sparked his interest. Well, I guess today was a little different. The conversation changed to something of his liking, and he began to speak up more often. He began to quite enjoy himself after a while. He was engaged in the conversation, appearing calm and content. Not that he wasn't typically calm and content. This time, something was...different. After a while, I caught myself and noticed I was staring intently at him. I was drawn to him, even though he was doing a very mundane action: talking. I scanned his face and noticed how he was smiling and laughing. Once again, these are very typical things. Nothing out of the ordinary. But today felt different. I felt different. It was as if I was looking at him for the first time. Or the first time I really looked at him.

I was feeling happy that he was feeling happy. That he was enjoying himself. But it was more than that. Somehow on that day, I was connected to him. Seeing him happy was creating joy in me. And that happiness within him radiated all over his face. His facial features, the ones I saw every day, looked different and yet the same: more prominent, more nuanced. There was more depth to it, as if his features were an afterglow of his soul. His presence, face, and body seemed more meaningful to me at that moment. The features that I always knew were aesthetic and symmetrical connected to me more deeply. It was a strange and beautiful process to experience. I felt confused. How could someone I spent all this time with suddenly look different one day? I wasn't sure what to make of this. I wasn't sure what I was feeling at that moment. This felt like an attraction of some sort. *Emotional, maybe? Physical? Eh, not really.* And why did this experience feel vaguely familiar?

It wasn't until the morning afterward that I understood the familiarity. That night, I had a dream. In this dream, I was running across the fields to meet someone far away, but I couldn't see who it was until I was right in front of them. Yeah, it was Ethan. He smiled at me. Then I woke up.

Ah, yes, I remember. There had been a few other instances in my life where I knew someone for a while, and then I would have a dream about them and suddenly felt different. Distinctly, this dream pattern was vaguely romantic in nature, but not always and not entirely, yet it was intimate in the emotional sense. Usually, after I had the dream, I would develop semi-romantic feelings for the person in question. It varied in type: sometimes, I would develop a crush, not necessarily a romantic one, but a connection where I would want to spend all my time with this person. And other times, it would be more romantic but not sexual; once again, wanting to spend time with them, but in a different, more exclusive context. But this hadn't happened in a while, and it was so rare that I forgot it could happen from time to time. Plus, and I don't know about you, it sounded ridiculous to me. Weird and ridiculous. I was almost annoyed with it: the idea of developing another set of feelings for someone after having a random romantic dream escapade with them. Is this how I became attracted to someone?

I didn't get it at all. The stranger part was that the dreams came more often after that, and most of them were again not sexual in nature. The most common recurring dream was one where Ethan and I were lying in bed together, fully clothed. He was just holding me. That's it. And I never felt safer or calmer. I was completely at peace and content. But when I woke up, I felt confused and guilty. Should I be dreaming about someone else's boyfriend? Most of the dreams were like that; Ethan comforting me with physical affection. After a while, they did become somewhat sexual. Maybe; I don't know. Even that process differed from what I was used to hearing from other people's sexual fantasies. In my waking state, I could not fantasize myself engaging in sex with him, not out of guilt per se, but I could not mentally picture it. I could think of the steps leading to some sort of sexual contact, but after that, my fantasies became fragmented, and the vision was blurred. As if it was hard to imagine myself being physical with him or with anyone. The thought of myself being sexual with someone was not satisfying to me. That was my typical line drawn with celebrities. As much as I bragged about wanting to have sex with them, I could never actually picture myself doing it. It wasn't being sex-repulsed as much as it was sex-blank, sex-neutral, sex-detached? And it wasn't low self-esteem either, like thinking I didn't deserve it. Which is why I enjoyed banter so much. I could engage in wordplay about sexual fantasies without actually having to picture myself doing it or engaging in it. That is how I could converse with peers about sex and enjoy it. It was more like a game of words, something detached from my person and a humorous topic to discuss but not physically partake.

I have a sneaking suspicion that some folks here think I am in denial. Perhaps some folks think I was always sexually attracted to Ethan, and I didn't want to admit it. Yeah, but no.

First of all, fuck you for not having faith in me being true to myself. Don't we know each other well by now? Also, this was a different scenario, something I could not talk about openly to other people because I have never heard anyone else experience things in this way. So I assumed they wouldn't get it. I would have had no issue noticing Ethan being sexually attractive from the jump. He wasn't dating Jacq right away, so there would be no guilt in my acknowledging and pursuing that option if it presented itself. You need to understand that these deep feelings or emotional attraction took me completely by surprise.

Who could I talk about this with? And who would believe me? Like one of my favorite Pitbull and Ying Yang Twins songs, they would scream, "Mentirosa, Mentirosa! Dale huevo, Dale huevo..." Fuck, that's not what I meant. It felt so complicated to understand myself, let alone explain to someone else. Maybe I should just keep tabs on this for a while. Give it some time to understand how I feel and what I want. Despite what was changing for me, I knew I still wanted to maintain our friendship. I wanted him to be part of my life as a friend. That was important to me. More important than this, for now.

Chapter Twelve // Passive-Aggressive Packages

So, you know how celebrities like to thank the Academy for their Oscar award? Well, I'd like to thank White women for teaching me the concept of passive-aggressiveness. Do you like me or nah? Choose one because you can't choose both! And I know that other people can also be passive-aggressive, but they're not part of this story, so...

The fact I have to keep saying something along the lines of "not all White BLANK" is part of the deeper problem here. Take it systematically, not personally, unless it is personal, then take accountability and don't be defensive about it. Plus, I never said I hated you. (Social justice me is shouting from the backstage wings...)

The truth of the matter is that certain women are socialized to be passive-aggressive in expressing their true feelings. Research has long confirmed that women are not given the same graces of being outwardly angry compared to men. The fact that it has to be confirmed through written research instead of taking women at their word is another frustrating argument in itself. However, despite those consequences, other women continue to express their anger and disagreement in public spaces. It goes back to truth vs. harmony. Unfortunately, some women have internalized their inability to acknowledge their anger so much that it comes out in passive-aggressive ways. This isn't an excuse for their behavior. It's still a bitch move. I cannot tell you how many times I've googled this term over the years after learning about it through Jacq. And I'm still confused about what it is and how it shows up. But it was also a very common behavioral pattern, almost normal. With this behavior, there's always the conversation about intentionality. Many experts say that many people do not even realize they are being passive-aggressive. It is so internalized that it becomes second nature. They do not have the chance to even realize they are upset until it

seeps   out   in   another   way.[9]
(https://www.racialhealthequity.org/blog/twofaced)

I learned about passive-aggressiveness the hard way while living with Jacq. It's not something you notice right away. That's the whole point: if people caught on immediately, it would be easier to challenge and confront, and the perpetrator would have to take responsibility. This maladaptive pattern serves two other functions. First, it allows the underlying issue or problem to be dragged on for longer. If someone does something to upset you, and you cannot confront it at the moment, or even worse, the perpetrator creates an environment in which it would be harmful to do so, either through authority or gaslighting, then yeah, you would want to get back at them. You might be tempted to make them suffer and prolong it as punishment. In some situations, I could completely understand that tactic, especially when the perpetrator is being abusive and you can't fight back.

The issue with passive aggression is that the behavior pattern responds to all types of uncomfortable and upsetting situations, even if the person who triggered the response did not deserve it... The assumption in using passive aggression is that the person feels justified in doing so. That they interpreted the situation correctly, and that the person who triggered the response did it maliciously and intentionally. Now, this is a bit different from the idea of intention vs. impact. A prime example of the latter concept is a person who accidentally steps on someone else's toes. They may have done it accidentally, but the other person got hurt, so they should take responsibility for it. This example is used to describe instances where someone unintentionally says something prejudiced or racist out of ignorance, not malice. In the end, it does not matter if the person was not being

---

[9] "Collins Airhihenbuwa asks "Is being 'two-faced' cultural, racial and/or gendered?" (racialhealthequity.org/blog/twofaced)

intentional, the hurt is done. Even if they did not realize, for example, that they used an offensive word, they have to take responsibility for the fact that they harmed another person with those words. The remedy is to apologize and educate themselves, so it does not happen again.

This also goes beyond the idea of whether a person is good or bad. Let me take a pause here because this is where most people get caught up. If you take nothing else from this book, it's this: good people, even the greatest, nicest people, can do terrible things to other people. It is a hard fact that we all have to accept if we are to deal with these uncomfortable situations. So why am I bringing this up? Since everyone can be passive-aggressive at some point, there's no room to argue whether someone is good or bad. Plus, that conversation takes away from the events that truly happened. If Mother Theresa accidentally stepped on my toes, should we get caught up on whether or not she's a good person? And folks telling me over and over again about how good of a person she is does not take away from the fact that she stepped on my toes. Good people are capable of doing wrong and terrible things all the time.

I've also noticed that passive aggression can come from misinterpreting the situation at hand, thereby punishing folks for no justifiable reason... That is the second unintended function. The trigger could be an action toward the person, or it could also be something in the environment itself that makes that person uncomfortable. Let's say that a person tells someone, "Nice shoes." In that person's mind, they meant it as a compliment, but if the triggered person misinterprets it as a sarcastic insult, then boom: trouble time. Now the triggered individual will become passive-aggressive for a reason that is not justified. Let's say that a person interprets something happening in the environment around them as uncomfortable or upsetting to them. Once again, the passive-aggressive response is unjustified. This, unfortunately, is the world where Jacq's subversive emotions thrived.[10]

Now, I'm not a saint. I may have, on many occasions, said something upsetting to folks, including Jacq. I'll admit it: my verbal discourse was often borderline (and over the line), criticizing, and abusive for a very long time. That's a hard pill to swallow and acknowledge in oneself. It is hard to acknowledge as a Black woman because I can see folks using it as justification for the "angry Black woman" stereotype to be used and overgeneralized based on this situation. Newsflash to the wise: this is not what this discussion is about. Open your eyes and mind beyond the stereotype and into the world of complex human behaviors and feelings. It took me years to realize that one of the main ways I dealt with childhood bullying, social exclusion, and racial microaggressions was to become an expert in verbal thrashing. Not to justify, it was still wrong. By the time I was in high school, I had become one of those folks who people know not to dish it out if they couldn't take it. Okay, maybe I didn't have a widely-known reputation, but people who interacted with me daily knew that I could be very harsh with the put-downs. It turned from reasonable responses to other people's bullying and aggressive behaviors to my go-to-response whenever I was angered, even just irritated. Most of the time, I did not realize how my words could be technically considered verbally abusive, albeit on the lower end of the spectrum, but unhealthy nevertheless (Gottman got me to realize that; thanks, White communication researchers).

Eventually, anyone could be in my path: friends, teachers, my baby sister (and I mean, my elementary-aged sibling while I was in high school), and even my parents. (behind their backs, of course. Even I knew my limits; if I said one word out of line, my ass was kicked out of the house.) Out

---

[10] "Dear White Women: Here's Why It's Hard to Be Friends With You" (aninjusticemag.com/dear-white-women-heres-why-it-s-hard-to-be-friends-with-you-61ba6e497f1a)

of all the people I attacked with my vicious discourse, my sister was the one that I eventually regretted the most. She was the relationship that eventually led to me reevaluating and changing my ways of communication in adulthood. I still haven't caved into maturity yet and told her all of this, of course. I mean, I know it's the right thing to do, but also, I don't want her to get a big head about it and do the whole "I told you so" bit. That shit is annoying, no matter how old the person is. Yes, I get it. I'm a terrible person sometimes. You know you still love me, though. World of readers and listeners. I grow on ya, like moss on a tree. Strangely rough yet beautiful. Or like in-laws. Just strange...but yet, here we are.

Maybe deep down inside, somewhere in my subconscious, I accepted this passive-aggressive behavior because I knew that I was not a great communicator myself. I knew that I had struggles with expressing my feelings, and on some level, I was able to acknowledge my snappiness as being unproductive, even if I could not fully see yet that it was unhealthy/abusive-lite. Nevertheless, even though I was prone to throw criticisms and lashings unintentionally from time to time, I did not deserve to be the recipient of passive aggression. No one deserves that. Neither type of behavior was right or justified. Yet, in those cases, when I was thrashing out and unintentionally hurting someone's feelings, I would have wanted to be corrected then and there. Coming from a culture and region where directness was valued, I did not mind being called out. I often thought that arguments should be out in the open. If you said something upsetting to me and I said something back, I was expecting a full-on direct conversation about it. But that's not where passive aggression lives. And yet, it was a direct result of Ethan's and I growing relationship and Jacq's discomfort with it. But I never knew how uncomfortable she was because she never outwardly said anything. That's the problem. Passive aggressiveness is a result of not being able to handle or own one's feelings. It was an issue with personal accountability of anger. That was so different from what I was used to growing up. I remember countless stories of teens in high school getting into it with someone because they acted out of line.

"Don't talk to my man!"

"I don't like it when you're hanging around them like that."

"If you loved me, you wouldn't be talking to *those girls*."

I fully admit that those statements and the underlying beliefs are highly problematic and controlling. No one should tell someone who they should be hanging out with. But at least folks knew if a person had an issue with it. I guess that is what I was looking for. An indication that someone was uncomfortable. That Jacq was uncomfortable with our relationship even though she could not force someone to choose who to spend time with. As long as there was no cheating, folks had the right to spend time with whoever they considered a friend. And come to think about it now, if Jacq expressed that discomfort, there was a part of me that would not care. And still, that part fluctuates in size and intensity.

Ethan and Jacq's relationship was a slightly unconventional one. I remember Jacq clearly stating at one point that they "never go on dates." She was right. It was very rare for them to go out together, just the two of them. Our squad would spend time with each other all the time, sort of like group dates, but there was technically only one couple. I thought that was how they liked it. It was different, for sure, but I enjoyed it because I was part of it. I learned years later that this was called *enmeshment*. I was enmeshed in their identity as a couple and I didn't even know it. We should have discussed setting boundaries, carving time as a group, and time for them as a couple. But then again, teenagers, amirite? And how could anyone expect a person prone to passive aggression to have an open, assertive discussion about boundaries?

Despite this hidden, underlying tension, I loved spending time with them. Hear. Me. Out. (Or read me out.) Love is complicated. I would say that the passive-aggressiveness, though poignant and potent when it did appear, was just a fraction of my interactions with Jacq, at least in the beginning. It was through Ethan and Jacq that I watched countless movies and played countless games. Socializing and bonding through media were important to me. I had a hard time opening up to people, so media and gaming provided an avenue for me to express myself and bond with others. I didn't have to think; I could just play. I didn't have to worry about being vulnerable because other people were being silly with me. That meant a lot to me, being able to just be my quirky self-engaging in expressive activity. It may seem trivial to others, but it was EVERYTHING to me.

I was terrible at them, but I loved playing those violent video games or even spending hours watching others play them. I knew it was weird at the time to enjoy watching other people play games for hours. But then Twitch came out several years later, and I was like, "Finally, my people! I'm not the only one!" Ethan and Jacq also introduced me to the concept of binge-watching. Gosh, I am showing my age here. Before the land of streaming platforms, folks had to go out of their way to acquire seasons of shows to watch them. I'm talking about waiting until those seasons were released on DVD, waiting for the marathon rerun day before the next season was going to air, or roaming the internet to find random sites that had multiple seasons together in one playlist. Wow, we had to work hard back then.

So, that's how I bonded with them. Ethan or Jacq would introduce me to a new show, and we would spend hours watching the episodes. At first, I thought we were all in agreement with this arrangement of which show we would watch together. But after a while, there were times when

Ethan and Jacq would watch episodes without me, and I would be left behind. Those included situations where I could not necessarily catch up myself since I did not have access to it. I was saddened by this, but I thought it was a harmless mistake. Maybe they got so excited that they went ahead without me. Sometimes I would go to sleep before them, so I thought they were tempted to continue. But it started to happen too often, to the point that I was missing whole shows.

Now, I can maybe sense what some folks are thinking. Maybe they wanted some time alone, you know, as a couple. That sounds like a reasonable explanation of things. Completely justified. It still hurt me like a motherfucker. It also felt like, deep inside, Jacq got some pleasure from doing this. Plus, if I may interject, you would think that if she truly valued our binge time together, she would have articulated her need to sometimes watch as a couple versus a group. It appeared as if I valued that time as a group much more than she did. It felt like a hierarchy of needs, too: my need to binge-watch as a group took a back seat to their couple time. That my needs were not as important since I was not fucking someone in the group. We both had our reasons for why we felt the way we did.

Oh, I completely forgot to mention how I learned the term "passive-aggressive." Or how I learned that is what Jacq was doing. It was from Ethan himself. One day, we were sitting together in the living room, and the topic of emotions came up. Robert was talking about anger and asking how people know if someone else is upset in a relationship.

Then Ethan chimed in, "Well, you can never tell if Jacq's angry because she's super passive-aggressive about it."

Jacq sat in silence. She turned her head slightly, squinted her eyes, and peered into Ethan's soul.

Ethan shifted his body and head and gave a nervous smile. He whispered in her ear, "Sorry, but you are passive-aggressive."

Jacq still said nothing, and eventually, the topic changed.

I had heard of the term maybe once before, but I had no idea what it meant. And the funny thing was, her reaction was the classic passive-aggressive response. As an outsider, she gave a look that said something like, "I'm not going to forget this."

Side note, the only time I recall Jacq giving an outwardly upset response came months later. I don't even know what the full conversation was about since I was not part of it. We were all in the common room, and I was sitting opposite some other folks. Even though I could not hear them, it looked like Jacq was upset about something, and Ethan was trying to get her to talk about it. I heard little snippets of words here and there, about food, dinner, or something like that. But she would not admit she was upset, at least not then and there. Then out of nowhere, she said, "Well, since I'm sucking your dick, I feel like I deserve at least one of YOUR chicken wings."

Hot damn. That came out of nowhere. I almost second-guessed myself if what I heard was real. But then again, why would I make up that phrase in my head? I suddenly had all the questions in my mind. I wanted to know more but felt out of place to ask. And honestly, I thought it was the blackest response I had heard from a White girl at the time. I was like, "Yes, you tell him!" But I didn't say that. I was happy she was upset. It was hilarious. That's the fire; that's the person I remember meeting and knowing once before. Where did she go?

Slowly over time, I got the sense that Jacq was becoming annoyed with my presence. It got to the point that all I had to do was enter the room, and she would make a loud sigh. But she was smart about it. She did it in a way that I couldn't tell if it was toward me or someone else in the room. The biggest case of her passive aggression towards me involved *shipping packages*. Yup, you heard that right. It doesn't make sense.

I already had an account with the student-run moving company where I would ship packages to my home on the East Coast. Jacq was aware of this and my positive experiences with it, so she asked me one time to use my account to ship some of her packages home along with mine, and she would pay me back for her part. As I think of this story now, I wonder why she didn't just get an account for herself. No, I must be forgetting something. There was a specific justifiable reason why she needed mine. I just can't remember. She had several ones of different sizes and weights, so I was trying to figure out how much everything would cost for her. I remember the process being very tedious and nerve-wracking for me. I wished someone from the company could have helped me. I nervously calculated what I thought was the final cost and gave it to Jacq. A little while later, I realized that my math was all the way fucked up. It was wrong. "So wrong," *said in Cady Heron's voice from Mean Girls.* Instead of correcting me on the spot, Jacq said nothing. For days. I didn't hear a word from her. No communication, text, email, nothing. Where's my money? After I finally realized my error, I felt ashamed. I immediately recalculated the cost and emailed her the updated one. Then she responded, "Yeah, that sounds like the right price," and sent me her check.

Why? Why did it have to get to that point for her to say something? And the tone of it read like I was trying to pull a fast one on her. That's why I felt ashamed. I already felt self-conscious about my math skills, and I also came from a background where fairness, especially around money, was sacred. I would never try to make someone pay me more than they owe. So that flippant, privileged response pissed me off. I also began to notice all the subtle behaviors up until then. Like when I picked up the boxes for her belonging and came over to give them to her. She made an audible sigh, rolled her

95

eyes, and walked out of the room after I presented it to her as a reminder to pack her things. Like when I walked into her having a phone conversation with a family member about travel plans to see them and overheard her saying that she was excited to get to see them because she needed to leave here. And then her huffing and puffing after I heard her having trouble getting a ride to the airport, and I offered to help her out. As if the idea of us riding together was too much for her.

I just about had it with her. It was clear that she was upset with me at that point, but she would never admit it or tell me why. What power she had over me, with the lack of acknowledgment, almost gaslighting in nature. I had to find out what was going on. If I wasn't going to get answers from her, I thought of the next best thing. One night, I headed over to speak to Ethan about it.

I asked him plainly, "Did I do anything to upset Jacq? She seems like she's mad at me for something."

Ethan paused to take a breath and sat down on the couch. I sat next to him. "No, she's not mad at you." The way he said it made me think there was something more behind it, but he wasn't giving much detail. At least by the tone, he acknowledged that I wasn't all the way crazy for thinking about it. But then again, he was denying it for her. I didn't push on it. Even though he said she wasn't upset with me, I knew he was lying. It may have been a ride-or-die move for his relationship, but it was a painful cut for me. We were also alone, one of the rare times in a long time. And while I wanted to take advantage of this time to catch up with him one-on-one, the looming darkness of Jacq's hold filled the room with despair. Once again, that subtle power tainted another bonding moment for me. I think she liked it that way.

Throughout this story, it is easy to paint a picture of villain vs. victim. But I don't like ascribing labels like that. It's one thing to not condone a pattern of behaviors and another to completely villainize someone. That's another part of my shame. I did not want to hate this person despite her making it so easy to do so. I thought I was doing something wrong by being involved in their group. I felt guilty for having desires and needs for connection with folks of different genders. I hated myself for starting to fall in love with him over time. I felt ashamed for having a deep connection with a man that fell outside and in between a romantic relationship. I thought my need for friendship took a back seat to a romantic relationship, and I resented society for reinforcing that belief. I'm not letting her off the hook, either. Jacq fucked up on me more than once. I don't forget that shit. I also believe we are both victims here. Victims of a society that is telling us how to deal with our emotions. I come from a family and culture where emotions were put out there, especially anger. Yes, there was always the overarching belief that you should be respectful to your parents and older family members. That also meant that you were not allowed to show anger toward your parents as a child. However, it was acceptable and even welcomed to openly express anger and discontent toward others, especially towards injustice. If something was going on that was not right, we spoke up about it and with each other. Now that I think about it, most of our conversations centered on us being upset about something that happened. But I thought that was normal. I wonder what White people talk about. Do they often have conversations about upsetting things happening in the world? Or are their conversations centered on maintaining peace or not being so outwardly expressive?

It took me a long time to learn the cultural and gendered differences in communication and how it boils down to the regulation of emotion. That is to say, society has a fucked up way of conditioning us as women to regulate our emotions in public. But what I have noticed is that women of color, particularly Black women still take the risk of openly expressing ourselves and our discontent. For myself, I don't necessarily see it as taking a risk. I see it as being honest, open, and authentic. If something fucked up is happening to me or someone I know, Imma say something about it. Period.

I cannot and will never completely understand it from a White woman's perspective. I can never truly understand the pressure of maintaining peace to the point of hiding one's true feelings or, even worse, not acknowledging or being aware of how one truly feels. And this is all centered on negative feelings because, of course, they are not going to get punished for openly expressing happiness and contentment. Case and point: can you ever imagine people getting openly upset at someone announcing their pregnancy or engagement? No. I get fucking annoyed at those announcements, but I wouldn't dare openly state my discontent in a public setting or face getting excommunicated from society. But openly talk about upsetting issues like racism and oppression? Have you ever tried to do that in a room full of White people? White women? Silence. That's the trick. I think people of color know that the quickest way to get White folks to shut up in public is to change the topic to race or racism (because those are 2 separate things--not all talk about race is a bad thing).

Negative emotions are warning signs. They alert us to something in the environment that we don't like and don't like how it's affecting us. And if we deny those emotions, they are just going to keep coming back. Spoiler alert: you can't skip the process of feeling emotions. They will catch up to you sooner or later. You have to acknowledge at some point that you feel uncomfortable. Sad, anxious, upset, angry.

Alright, White women. I hope you're not still thinking that I hate you. Just a temperature check. If you feel like you are getting read, well, sit with it. It's not an attack. And I'm reading myself too. I think people get upset when they think things are hitting a little too close for comfort. "We're not supposed to be talking about things like this. It sounds too close to me." Like shining a mirror in your face. I'm shining a mirror on myself too.

I hope that we can get to a point in our society where White women can comfortably express their anger in public. Not feel like they have to agree or stay silent to keep the peace and harmony. That we as a society can get over the fact that just because someone is angry doesn't mean it is directed toward you. And even if it was, you can sit with that discomfort. That you don't have to jump to feeling like you are a bad person because it has nothing to do with that. Good people can be good and still do fucked up things. Happens all the time.

Quoting my bad-ass colleagues of color, anger is a great emotion. Being angry is not a bad thing. How you respond to that anger is the real issue. And that means beyond acknowledging and expressing that you are angry. It's okay to do that. It's not okay to yell, fight, or punish others, directly or passive-aggressively. Anger and feelings of upset serve a great function, typically because it is a result of injustice: it shows that we care about ourselves being treated well and let us know that we like ourselves enough not to be taken for granted.

This is stating the obvious, but I hope we can get to a point where we all can openly express anger and frustration in public. Because societal norms forcing us to suppress negative emotions harms everybody regardless of gender, race, etc. And allowing only certain kinds of people the right to be openly angry harms every single body because we know even with those in power, it still comes with stipulations.

So yes, Jacq. You have every right to be openly upset about not getting that chicken wing. No matter how weird that statement sounds... But don't take that shit out on me. *Remember that.*

Chapter Thirteen // The Cross-Country Camping Trip from Hell

Sometimes in life, you make stupid decisions. Going on a camping trip with White people was mine. Okay, it probably didn't matter if they were White or not. Camping just sucks. What's worse is that I invited myself on this camping trip with White folks. They stereotypically yet correctly assumed that it would NOT be a good fit for me, but alas, my desire to be included in their group superseded my common sense. I should have known it was a bad idea when Ethan introduced the trip via PowerPoint Presentation. Nerd. That is why my parents laughed hysterically when they discovered that their oldest daughter would be roughing it out in the wild. I strayed from the traditional college vacation to follow my friends on a cross-country camping trip to the Grand Canyon. It was a radical shift from what I was used to. I was a girl from the city, someone who had never set foot into the country. I never seemed to be interested in the outdoors. For this reason, my parents pleaded against such a random and perhaps rash decision.

A few months earlier, I sledded down a hill for the first time. It was not a giant hill, but I felt so happy to overcome my fear of heights. At first, I was unwilling to participate, but my friends convinced me to take a risk. I thoroughly enjoyed myself. From then on, I wanted to take more risks and try new things. So when I heard about my best male friends planning a trip to see the Grand Canyon, I wanted to join them.

My friends all had prior camping experience and therefore knew, for the most part, what to expect from the trip. Our entire group consisted of three men and two women. The core group, of course, was with Ethan, Robert, Jacq, and me. Then there was the new boy, Joaquin. The three boys, Ethan, Robert, and Joaquin, were especially close, though, and this trip seemed to be the perfect way to show off their outdoor survival skills. Jacq, so sweet and girly, was a different story. Although she had been camping before, I surmised she came mainly because of Ethan. She joined the trip out of romantic obligation. So, no matter what happened on the trip, I knew her motivations were to be as cooperative and lovable as possible so she could appear to be the ideal girlfriend. And though I openly talked about taking risks, I was unwilling to admit that I, too, had an underlying motivation.

I always considered my relationship with Ethan and Robert to be close, and I tried my best to keep the friendship strong. Nevertheless, I began to feel a strain when Joaquin, a new friend of theirs, became part of our group. He was very nice, and we soon found that we all had much in common. Even so, I could not help but realize how quickly all the men became close. They only knew Joaquin for a couple of months, yet they behaved like they had known each other for years... I, on the other hand, had known them much longer and had yet to become as close a friend as they were with him. Though satisfying, my friendship with Ethan and Robert was not nearly as great as I wanted it to be. Jacq was part of that wedge between Ethan and me. But even with that, my gender and lack of romantic connection with either of them prevented me from becoming their best friend. My being a woman created a barrier that stopped me from being as close a friend as another man. And I *hated* that.

It saddened me to come to such a realization, but I envisioned this camping trip as an opportunity to not only bond with my friends but also prove where I stood in terms of our friendship. I hoped that participating in a cross-country journey – something unfamiliar to me but familiar to all of them – would prove that I was resilient. So even though on the outside it appeared that I was a risk-taker, on the inside, I wanted their approval and acceptance of me as a "bro."

On that note, I began to help them acquire things for the trip. The first thing we set out to find was a car. We tried to rent a car but found that the minimum age to do so was twenty-five. Because we were all underage, we had to look for another option. Robert happened to live in the area and was able to get a car from his parents. They did not trust us with their fancier car, so they loaned us their Toyota Prius. I was not familiar with the model at the time and did not think twice about it until I saw its strange beauty with my very own eyes.

It was a hybrid, which was good since it was designed not to hurt the environment. Unfortunately, it was also designed to hurt my feelings. Though silver and gorgeous inside and out, it was extremely small, not far from the size of a clown car. To make matters worse, we had to reduce the number of supplies due to its size. Since the food and the tent were considered to be of utmost importance, the materials we chose to get rid of were some of our clothes. It was a last-minute decision, so I did not have a chance to notice what I was giving up until much later in the trip. My position in the car was inconvenient as well. From the beginning, I told my friends that I was not planning to drive. The reason for this is simple: I am terrified of driving. Beyond fear, the idea of getting lost in a foreign place concerned me. I hoped they would understand. They did, but as a compromise for not driving, they said that I had to sit in the middle seat in the back of the car while everyone else rotated positions. It seemed like a good compromise at first, but then I realized that I would be sandwiched between Ethan and Robert, who were beautiful but exceptionally giant in stature, for a great portion of the trip. Just to take my mind off the discomfort, I brought my homework with me, which only seemed to take up even more unwanted space in the car.

The day we left was a warm, lovely Friday afternoon, and I was in high spirits. After my morning class, we gathered our final belongings and loaded them into the car. This day was the longest in terms of the amount of time we had to drive to get to our first destination: Boulder, Colorado, in thirteen hours. One special part of that day, which stood out to me, was at night when we sailed through the long, giant cornfields.

My friends took the liberty to entertain themselves by singing to a playlist of over one hundred cheesy Disney songs. While they sang in glee, I was speechless. It was Jacq's playlist, and while I'm sure she picked it out of her sheer love for it, I also believe there was a hidden agenda to torture me with it. I was getting used to enjoying chick flicks, but even I had my limits. I like a mixture of things, not to be inundated by childlike overstimulation. The only reason I didn't jump out of the car was that we were literally in the middle of nowhere Kansas.

We arrived at a friend of Robert's house in Colorado late. He kindly let us stay at his place for the night, and we were all ready to get some well-deserved sleep. I remember being a little disappointed and nervous, lying on a hard floor in my sleeping bag. Looking back, I now realize that it was the best night of sleep I had during the entire week. Well, almost. I noticed that Jacq and Ethan got to share a sleeping bag. And while I was in no way envious about sharing that tiny ass bag, I was a bit upset that they were able to get a moment of intimacy, the type of intimacy that was socially accepted only because they were a couple. That night, like many other countless nights, I was skin-starved. Normally I could have dealt with it better since I was on my own, but I was irritated by the fact that this time around other people were enjoying physical affection and comfort in my presence. On the other hand, the fact that we were indoors and in a heated room did not seem like a luxury to me when it should have been.

The next two days were entirely dedicated to being spent in a national park located in Utah. The drive there was also long; when we arrived, it was nightfall. Completely exhausted, I almost forgot that we did not eat dinner yet. It was too late, however, to search for wood to build a fire. Frustrated, I took matters into my own hands and grabbed a can of tomato soup and a can opener. Before I realized what was happening, I had ingested about half the can of uncooked soup. Jacq stared at me with a face full of disgust. It was only the second night out, and I was already behaving like a barbarian. My eyes were wild with intensity, and my stomach

103

was only half full. I did not think anything could get worse, that is, until I stepped inside our tent for the night.

The tent was huge: it had enough space for the five of us with plenty of extra room. We grabbed our clothes from the car and started to change in front of each other. It was not as awkward for me because I put more clothes on top of what I was wearing. What bothered me was the brutally cold weather. I was still shivering, even with many layers of clothing on. My sleeping bag added no comfort to the situation. I was not an expert in buying camping supplies, especially sleeping bags, so I used the only one I had. It was a small, 50-degree bag that I bought a while ago for my pre-orientation weekend. I stupidly thought that 50 degrees meant that wherever you slept, the temperature inside that bag would be 50 degrees. I later found that the bag was meant to be used only in 50-degree weather. Every night that week was about 30 degrees. My friends knew I was not accustomed to this weather, so they provided me with another solution, spooning.

Now, you would assume by my previous comments of being skin-starved that I would be ecstatic to spoon with my friends. However, this was not an ideal situation for comfort. It was so cold that I couldn't even enjoy or was aware of the physical affection, and more importantly, the only reason they volunteered to help me out was to prevent me from freezing to death. It felt more like a concession due to an obligation. So I chose life over death and let Robert hold me for the night, which sounded better than it was. I wonder how Ethan and Jacq handled the night. Oh yeah, they both had individual sleeping bags that were warm, and they got the chance to spoon on top of that. Me, jealous? I don't know her.

Amazingly, I managed to survive to see the next day. I did not recall falling asleep, but soon enough I was awakened by the bright, glowing streaks of sunlight shining through the tent. The day had come, and it was now time to explore the national park. I have never hiked in my lifetime, but I was so empowered by the fact that I made it through such a bad night that I felt I could do anything. It was also much warmer during the day, and I forgot how cold I had been the night before. We grabbed our water bottles and snacks and ventured past the campgrounds and into the hiking trail. The scenery was incredibly breathtaking. Large, unique rock formations towered above us and into the horizon. We climbed on top of a small mountain and looked down at an amazing view of the ground. I felt like I was on Mount Everest. Clearly, I didn't understand how geography works.

Sooner than I anticipated, night had crept upon us again. I tried as hard as I could to avoid going inside the tent. I took a detour and walked around the campground, noticing the many giant RVs. They seem so magnificent to me, so enticing. How I longed to be inside one, just for a moment. To be surrounded by warmth and possibly good food. Perhaps there would be a television inside, and I could catch up on my favorite shows. If only my wish were granted. Ethan spotted me staring at the large vehicles. I told him that I wished we were in one. He looked at me oddly and dismissed such a notion. He and his other manly comrades preferred to use as little technology as they could while camping. They wanted to stay true to the natural elements. Readers and listeners, how do you politely tell your White friend that he's a dumbass? I saw the practicality of using an RV, especially when it came to being sheltered from the cold. We could all still be "manly" and warm at the same time.

We began to argue, and I may have exchanged some not-so-kind words. Have you ever engaged in an argument where you questioned another person's sanity? Back then, I dealt with conflict in some unhealthy ways: mainly name-calling, interrupting, criticism, etc. I have since changed and learned to be a more effective listener and communicator, but back in the day? Shit, you had to be thick-skinned to last in battle with me. I'm sure it resulted from decades of bullying, gaslighting, and learning to be tough as a result, but my way of coping with conflict during those times was not better or healthy at all. After a while of Ethan and I engaging in an intense discussion, we agreed to disagree.

That night, I prepared myself for another terrible cold bout of sleeplessness. As we were all getting settled into our sleeping bags, I overheard what sounded like night talk, the type of talk between lovers. *What the fuck? Can't I just suffer in peace?* I was surprised, too, since I had not seen Ethan and Jacq talk that way in front of me, or at least in a long time. Before I knew it, they leaned into each other for a goodnight kiss. *Ugh.* I was frozen and still. This was the first time I saw them kiss each other. It was shocking. My response shocked me more. I did *NOT* like it at all. I was uncomfortable and upset. Then the guilt set in. Why should I be upset at them? They are together after all, and I thought that I was confident I did not like Ethan that way. It felt like jealousy, and I was not ready to accept that. Accepting I had romantic feelings for Ethan made this situation much worse. He was my friend, and I wanted to keep it that way. I did not want to give in to those other feelings because it would mean that Jacq was right. That her passive-aggressive behaviors were justified because I did like him. Or love him. *Shit, I don't know. I never went into this with the intent of falling for anyone, let alone trying to compete and ruin a relationship.* The vast majority of the time, my feelings for Ethan were friendly. Now here we are, after months and months of friendship, and these other complicated feelings are bubbling to the surface? Was I lying to myself before? I don't think so. But I didn't think anyone would believe me if I told someone. If I was attracted to Ethan, wouldn't I have realized it from the beginning? Sure, I knew he wasn't awful looking, but that's it. Plenty of people can be good-looking to me, but it didn't mean I was fully sexually attracted to them. And normally, the attraction was fleeting. *Was that not normal? Oh, goodness.* The grey was turning to color again.

Gosh, I could not tell a soul. I had to keep this to myself until I figured it out. I thought focusing on sleep would help me, but it didn't. Once while tossing and turning, I turned around

106

and saw Ethan's face facing me. I paused for a second before turning around again. I noticed how peaceful his face was while asleep. *Aw, that's sweet,* I thought. *No! OMG, what am I thinking?* I turned around quickly and covered my face. I had to forget that. But then again, it's normal to casually notice someone sleeping peacefully. It wasn't like I was staring at him for hours. You know what? It's so normal and not awkward that I bet I could mention it to him in the morning; how sweet and silly he looked asleep while I was tossing and turning. That wouldn't be weird, right? Well, folks, I did mention it, and he did find it weird. Face palm.

We were on the road again in the morning to another park in Utah. I tried not to pay attention to the road signs on the side of the mountains we crossed that said "Falling Rock" and "Deer Crossing" because they were increasing my already high level of anxiety. There were more trails to hike at the next park; however, these were more advanced. I believed I was prepared to conquer my fears until I saw a sign. I do not recall what it said verbatim, but it casually mentioned the risk of falling and death. Suddenly, my courage faded. I sat in the car and did some schoolwork while my friends risked their lives on the trial.

I was relieved when they came back alive. Still, I was not satisfied with my lack of risk-taking. My friends convinced me to hike on another trail, one less dangerous. I was terrified, but I accomplished the goal. Nevertheless, I could not get rid of the deep, sinking feeling of discomfort and uneasiness. Even though I had tried my best not to complain and be cooperative, I could not escape the fact that I did not want to be there. Robert stated earlier that day that he did not like when people complained about camping trips. I took this statement to heart partly because I wanted to prove that I could survive, not just because I was new to camping but because I was a woman and their female friend. Be that as it may, I knew I had my breaking point. And the kiss from the night before did not ease my mind. I realize now that I should have slammed Robert's remarks for their ignorance and complained. Suddenly, my friends, who I viewed as somewhat normal, were slowly becoming more irritating.

The rest of the trip was a blur. By the time we finally got to the Grand Canyon, I was exhausted. My male friends were just getting started with their day. I was glad to reach our final destination, to see the Grand Canyon, but I was not excited to walk along the side of the cliff, which is what they wanted. Walking down would have been too strenuous, so they said the midpoint was a good stopping place. Haziness and confusion filled my mind as we trekked our way down. I absolutely, positively did not want to go, but I put on a courageous mask to hide the anxiety. I coped with the situation by detaching my mind from my body to the point that I forced myself to not register what was happening. Still, I was tired and had to pause often in the middle of the trail. The boys thought it was a good thing to frequently stop because it allowed us to rest and drink water. Going up too fast would make us dehydrated. That is what they thought had happened to me that I became dehydrated. I did not want to appear emotionally weak, so I let them believe it was true.

When we took a break to eat lunch, the boys discovered the weather was going to be unpleasant for the night and chose to start driving back home a day earlier than planned. I was ecstatic to hear the great news. We intended to stop at a camping site in New Mexico, but we got lost on the way there. It was completely dark, and no camping ground was in sight. Being the manly men they were, the boys wanted to continue riding non-stop until we reached home. I wanted to go home more than anyone else, but I had a feeling that it would be a bad idea. And it was. Sitting in the back of a cramped car for twenty-four hours straight was not amusing at all. It was awful, even though we stopped a couple of times to stretch and to get food. Eventually, we were back on our college campus after the exceedingly long ride. I immediately ran up the stairs, into my suite, and climbed onto my bed. It felt so good to be in my bed again. Good fucking night.

My male friends did acknowledge how brave I was for camping with them shortly after our trip, especially when they knew I had such a horrible time. This is what I wanted to hear, or so I thought. I proved to Ethan, Robert, and myself that I was indeed strong, but I was wrong in trying to demonstrate my strength solely for their approval. So not feminist of me. Plus, it did not matter to them whether or not I could survive in the wilderness. Still, I persisted in proving that even though I was a girl, I could be just as tough as any man. Once again, my one-sided and skewed view of feminity was taking hold of me. Even if that were the only reason, it still did not make sense to me why I would take such a huge risk. Then I realized: it had to be something about the people I was going with that sparked such a strong devotion to friendship. I like to think that in addition to showing my strength, I went camping because I wanted to be with them. Ultimately, I wanted to show that despite our differences in outdoor activities, I was willing to go out of my comfort zone and risk everything because they were my friends.

I also was determined to create a space for myself within this friendship group. I did not like how I was pigeonholed in the current role in the friendship with these men. That as a woman, I could not be as close to them unless I was in a romantic relationship. I wanted more for myself. I deserved more for myself. This type of friendship was limited for me. And the trigger for my desperation to create space was seeing how easy it was for Joaquin to bypass the journey and forge a much more meaningful relationship with two people I had known for much longer than him. Women deserve to be more than just acquaintances or girlfriends. I wanted more for myself and them, but we deserve better. But then, I felt it all fall to shit when in the middle of this trip, I realized that my feelings were more complicated than I thought, at least with Ethan. It wasn't quite as platonic as I thought. And I had *no clue* how to deal with it.

Chapter Fourteen // Borderline Latina

On that fine spring day, relaxing in cool, blue water near the riverbank with Ethan, Jacq, and our other friends, I started to panic. *Holy crap!* I thought. *My Latin American theatrical production was about to premiere in less than one month! Could I truly handle being the co-chair of the annual college cultural show?* As soon as the panic came, it went out of my body and floated into the river. I still had time left to worry about my musical production later...back to my well-deserved vacation...

Ever since I learned in my high school history class that my family's country of origin was technically in Latin America, I was determined to embrace my Latin roots, and that exploration continued in college through my extracurricular activities. But I embraced that passion mainly in secret until and through high school out of concern that other people would invalidate me. After all, it is widely believed that folks from my parent's country do not *look* Latinx or Hispanic. But what did that mean anyway?

According to the standard definition, Latin America consists of countries once colonized by Spain. Our country was colonized by Spain, and Spanish is one of the many commonly spoken languages there. Also, I have always been low-key upset that the country literally adjacent to us has been accepted as part of Latin America with no questions asked. Do people not know that we were once all one country colonized by the same people (i.e., enslaved, murdered, forced into labor)? This border between the country has become a symbol of otherness for us. The fact that one side can claim that part of history and the other cannot is devastation. Also, not to be a political or historical downer (oh, fuck it), but American policies around Latin America always included our country. Look up the Monroe Doctrine, President Wilson-led forced military occupation, sugar-cane exploitation, etc. I know that a recent president has been getting a lot of buzz for his racist beliefs and actions, but trust me, President Wilson was the O.G. cunt on the spectrum of racist U.S. presidents. And lest not forget the Louisiana Purchase. Yeah, Arkansas would not exist if it weren't for our revolution that led our colonizer in desperate need of funds from the U.S. Google it if you want to explore more of what you never learned in history class.

It would take me several years to fully acknowledge the underlying factor in claiming this identity: anti-blackness, along with the inability of the world to acknowledge a former slave colony gained its freedom as the first in the world. The first Black and Latin American country to do so, I might add. But we were never truly acknowledged as a free nation because we were former slaves. We were forced to pay a freedom tax and to endure countless other countries invading our lands and stealing our resources, centuries after Spain.

Many folks also vehemently and fervently claim that being Hispanic or Latinx has a certain look. Many people do not realize (or don't care to accept) that Hispanic/Latinx is a linguistic designation, not a race-based one. Anyone of any race, culture, or ethnicity can be Latinx. Yet, when people think of that demographic, they think of White or fair-skinned people. I could go into the long history of colorism, pigmentocracy, and the overarching legacy of White supremacy that has created this whole oppression mess within our colonized cultures, but I won't. You get the subtext, and I trust that you can look up the other pieces to this historical-cultural puzzle. Let's get back to me.

When I started college, I wanted to get involved in student organizations, particularly cultural clubs. So I joined the Black Student Group and The Latinx Student Group. For a while, I could easily attend meetings for both clubs. After a while, however, I noticed that the meeting times overlapped for several weeks and eventually got to the point where they were in constant conflict. Both ran biweekly, but at the same time, on the same day. I felt like I had to make a choice: hang

111

with the Black kids or Latinx kids. I was confused and upset. Why did it have to be this way? And it felt like I was the only person affected by this conflict. While there were many times when folks from both clubs would attend the other club for special discussions and events, I was the only person I knew that was trying to consistently attend both.

I decided to abandon the Black Student Group to exclusively attend the Latinx Student Group. By the time I made the decision, it was a relatively easy one to make, but still not a comfortable one. I based my choice on how many people I interacted with and connected with during the meetings. The Black Student Group had a much bigger membership size than the other group. And it felt like the other first-years clicked with one another long before we started college. Remember that trip before college? It was a multicultural-themed pre-orientation in which most of the people who attended were also the ones who joined the Black Student Group. I did not get the chance to create a bond with as many people as my other Black peers, and it seemed as if they kept in touch over the summer through the start of our first year. I felt like I was left behind, like arriving late at a train station only to see the train moving away from me. And even though I was able to catch the next train that arrived shortly after, I could never catch up to that other train. Yet I could see the smiles on my peers' faces through the train window as it continued to cruise along slightly ahead of me.

The Latinx Student Group was *different*. The club was much smaller, and I was not the only first-year who did not know most other people. We had the opportunity to introduce each other, and through smaller group activities, I got to know those members better. So, I continued attending those meetings and had a great time going to different social and cultural events. The highlight event of this group each year centered on a major cultural celebration in the spring. I attended it once and fell in love with it. It was a play that had dance performances from Latin American countries. Admittedly, every major cultural club had a yearly theatrical show, but I liked ours the best. I was inspired enough to run in the election to chair the program. And folks, I won the election! But that came with a major responsibility of co-writing the play, auditioning the choreographers and dancers, and in my case, also serving as director. We had a cast of over 150 people. For many, it would be a terrifying challenge. Good thing for me: I like terrifying challenges.

My involvement in this theatrical production spanned several months. I never liked to be the center of attention and share the show's details with other people, including my squad. It wasn't an intentional exclusion, but now I realize I missed out on taking stock of the process and sharing the small beautiful details that led to a great production. I didn't think it was an option, a way to connect more with my friends by sharing my passions with them. While I didn't share all the behind the scene details, they were aware of the show and my roles in it. I'm not that modest. It wasn't until a few weeks before the show, while we were on vacation together, that they started to clearly see the anxiety on my face. While I was relaxing in the river in the warm Florida sun, it finally dawned on me that the show was around the corner.

"Are you excited that your show is coming up soon?" Ethan asked... I was hanging with the group of five, including him and, of course, Jacq.

"Yeah, I am." Then I paused to count the remaining days.

"Wow, I can't believe it's less than a month away." *Wow, where did the time go? Shit, I have so much more I should do. But chill, Pia. Remember why you went on this trip. It was perfect timing. A chance to get away from school and all the drama of planning the show. Look at the water and the clear sky. Soak it all in.*

This was the second friend trip we had together. The first one was way worse. I'm surprised I survived it. I almost murdered my friends in the woods…in the middle of bumfuck Kansas, no less. This time in Florida was a different story. We stayed at an actual house this time, Ethan's grandmother's place, in a lovely, quiet retirement town. We went to restaurants, a basketball game, and the beach. And of course, a float trip down the river. I saw a crocodile for the first and, fortunately, the only time. Everyone was getting along with one another and having a good time. Well, mostly. There were subtle hints of people getting frustrated or annoyed. But, hey. People go through different emotions all the time, and it doesn't have to do with me. Most of the time, I would be correct with that reasoning. But this time, it *did* have to do with me. I'm talking about Jacq because who else would I be talking about?

The first hint was at the beach. I was (and still am) self-conscious about my body, although back then, I was thin and had a natural set of abs. When we were at the beach, I revealed my physique in my bikini and short ensemble to the masses to great applause. Haha, no, that's not what happened. I uncomfortably changed in the horrible public restroom and rushed out so fast that I stumbled back onto the beach. No one saw or cared about it. I did not think it was a big deal because many people, including Jacq, were just as great looking in their swimsuits... Jacq and I complimented our outfits, and I accepted the exchange at face value. Then we went off to build sandcastles in the sand and stroll along the beach.

At one point, we started taking pictures. This was the time before selfie sticks, so we traded phones to take pictures of one another. Ethan wanted to take a picture with me. Jacq volunteered to take it for us. We stood next to each other and smiled. We looked happy. It was nice. Maybe it was too nice. Jacq snapped the pic and showed it to us. Well, Ethan looked nice. Me? Not so much. I was mostly okay, with the notable exception of my eyes being closed. She took the picture as I blinked.

A normal person who took the pic would have seen it and immediately tried to retake it, right? It was obvious. But Jacq did not say anything. She acted as if the picture looked fine. But it didn't look fine. There was an obvious, glaring mistake.

Have you ever been in a situation where you noticed something obviously wrong, so obvious that you'd think other people would notice, but no one says anything? And since no one says anything, you question and second-guess yourself? This was one of those times. However, during that time (and many, many times afterward), I second-guessed myself. Was there an issue? Was I making a big deal of things? Okay, maybe I am. I guess I won't say anything, then. After all, it wasn't a terrible picture.

That was the issue. Little did I realize that I default to questioning myself and giving others the benefit of the doubt in uncertain, vague situations like this. And I didn't realize that other people could notice and potentially take advantage of this. I now believe that is what Jacq did. It turned out to be a pattern. Remember how I said I could never truly tell what she was thinking? And while I found that quality mysterious, endearing, and attractive, it was also manipulative. Not only could she mask her true feelings, but she could also take advantage of ambiguous situations with passive-aggressive behavior. Or she could sense and take advantage of situations where people like me would internalize ambiguous actions from other people. Intentional or unintentional?

I don't know. Sometimes I think some folks' inability to deal with discomfort at face value makes life worse for everybody, including that person. Was she jealous that I was taking a picture with Ethan? What was wrong with friends wanting to take a picture together? This is probably why it was so hard for me to accept her jealousy. I cannot accept someone thinking it is not good for male and female friends to take pictures with each other. It was a simple ritual. I needed to have that. I needed to participate in some rituals without questioning whether I had the right to do so. It angered me to think that I had to give up so much to the point of no longer taking selfies with friends. No, I can't accept that. So, it made much more sense for me to think that I was overthinking things. That the picture was a mistake that she did not notice. So I let it slide. The next day, however, I could not ignore the signs of discontent.

Towards the end of our floating trip, we rested by a small river bank. My friends started to swim around, and I stood back, watching them.

"We're going to teach you how to swim," they said.

"Oh, no. That's okay." I said, nervously. Yeah, I know. Can't swim. I'm a fucking stereotype. Get over yourselves. Ethan swam over to me. "Don't worry. We're here to help you. You'll be fine."

"Okay, I guess I'll try." I started to entertain the idea. I readied myself for Ethan to start instructing me when Jacq came over.

"Here. I'll help you," she said gleefully.

She reached out her arms to signal that she was ready to lift and support my frame in the water.

Suddenly, a chill came over me. I couldn't explain it. She was standing there, calm and smiling, confident in her pose to teach me swimming. She said those words. They were kind and supportive. So why did I get very nervous at that moment? No one else looked concerned. They were waiting for me to jump and get started. I took another slightly longer look at Jacq's face. It looked calm, but I got the eerie sense of something sinister underneath. Right behind her eyes, I could see a glimmer of something deeper. A slight shift in the face said, "Sure, go ahead. If you hop on me, bitch, I'll *make sure* you'll drown."

Yikes! Where did that come from? That couldn't be what she was thinking. But why did that thought come into my mind? Before then, I was nervous, but I wasn't thinking that someone would try to sabotage me. Maybe I was overthinking things. Maybe it was because I was nervous. But that thought came out of nowhere. It didn't feel like a thought of my own.

I took a deep breath and trusted my instinct. Something was wrong here. *Don't move over to Jacq,* I thought. So, I recoiled myself, almost flinching, and said aloud, "Sorry, no thanks." I moved away.

"Are you sure?" They all looked at me, confused.

"Yeah, I'm sure."

From everyone's perspective, it was clear that I rejected Jacq's offer and felt uncomfortable. Jacq looked dismayed, losing face. But this is the kicker. It was her actions that led me to reject her. So why did it look like I was the bad one here? Like I was the one being rude and unappreciative? Ah, that was a clever tactic, I later learned. To be able to subtly behave in a way that makes another person react negatively, but that person ends up getting blamed for it. But at that time, I internalized those sorts of things to be my fault again.

I felt sorry for her. Not that I condone her actions. They were all the way wrong. But I hold a bit of sadness for someone who feels the need to engage in those underhanded ways because they were unable to sit with discomfort or negative feelings. It seemed intentional yet so automatic, like a learned pattern of just being in the world. That's the way that some people deal with uncomfortable subtext. Once again, they hate feeling anything negative or shameful, so much that it seeps out in underhanded behaviors that punish others. Could she have been just jealous of Ethan wanting to teach me how to swim? Something inside me was screaming. *No, it can't be that. So I can't take pictures or take swimming lessons from a friend? Where's the line?*

After that awkward encounter and reaction, we spent the rest of the vacation as if nothing had happened. And there was that. Soon enough, the vacation was over, and I had to go back to planning my big show. I remember the week of the show was extremely stressful. Just the sound of someone just breathing ticked me off. We had long rehearsals that ran late into the night. I was constantly thinking something would go wrong on the show. But I was still optimistic at my core, and after the rehearsals were over, I was more confident that things would run smoothly for our two-night performances.

A few weeks before the show, Jacq told us that her family would be visiting. *Cool,* I thought. *It's good that she gets to spend time with them.* Then I realized that her family would be in town the same weekend as the show. *Great,* I thought. *She would obviously bring them.* There was still plenty of time to buy tickets, and I know that Ethan and my other friends had already bought theirs for the second night, as well as other people on our dorm floor. Well, that could have also been the result of a very well-written promotional email from yours truly. I distinctly remember signing off with "Peace and hair grease" for some random reason. It did the trick. Anyway, as the event grew closer, I still heard no word from Jacq about her family's plans for that night. Maybe she was the type of person that does things last minute. I get it, sort of. But, I was so consumed with the show that I did not realize her stalling.

Then I got the news a couple of nights before. Jacq told me she and her family had other plans for that night. The way she phrased it, it seemed like it was an important event or something that just happened to be on the same night. It wasn't until after the show and I mean the following week that I learned she missed the show to go to the mall with her family. The fucking mall. The one that had always been there and we went to all the time. And no, it wasn't a special mall. The East

118

Coast girl in me would understand missing a show to go to a rare or exquisite mall with fancy once-in-a-lifetime special events. But no, it was a basic mall, and now that I think about it, I'm pretty sure they had all been there before.

Who does that? And what type of parent would agree to do that? Yeah, I'm shit-talking the parents. Honestly, what kind of explanation could a child give to justify her missing a major event for a friend? Did she say I fucked her boyfriend, or did she even mention the event to them? Did they know what truly happened? I don't want to disrespect her parents, but my parents have always been thoughtful of my friends, even those who did messed-up things to me. They would be like, "I know she's annoying, but how's so-and-so?" This made me think: *did her folks even know about me at all*?

Out of all the things Jacq did to me, missing the show hit me the hardest. I didn't care that she would often not wait for me to head over to dinner with the guys or that she sometimes didn't advocate for me to be included in certain hang outs. These are things that annoyed me for sure, but once again, I thought I was overreacting. Maybe she just likes to walk fast like them, and I just needed to catch up. Or maybe it wasn't her responsibility to bring me up when the guys were planning events when I wasn't around. I was slightly more lenient in those situations because I felt like the boys were at fault too. Why didn't they wait for me as well? Why didn't they naturally include me in their group outings?

And to tell you the truth, I was included in almost all of our outings; these were more like exceptions to the rule. Oh, and the fucking birthday pity cake. I wanted to celebrate my birthday that one time, but everyone magically forgot... She surprised me with a cake the day afterward, but even then, she made me feel guilty that I wasn't happy about it. Her cheers felt cold with subtext, and the cake was soaked in that taste.

There was another layer to her decision that further invalidated me. I was still self-conscious about being a Black co-chair of a Latin American production. Even though I am Latina, I was still concerned that people wouldn't take me seriously as the leader of this program. That concern was mainly towards people outside of my cultural group. Luckily, my fellow club members accepted me for who I was, no questions asked. So, when Jacq decided not to come, she probably thought she was just taking a jab at a project of mine because she didn't like how it was strengthening the bond between Ethan and me. Throughout this process, he was eager to learn more about my show and checked in with me every so often for more details. Clearly, he was interested in it, and Jacq considered him even more interested in me by extension.

But what she failed to realize is that her absence of support in my production was not just one of many projects of mine; it was a part of my identity. By not engaging in that side of me, she was invaliding a part of my identity, a part I was so desperately trying to embrace myself and show others. Oh, it's just a show, she probably thought. She might have surmised that Pia is involved in so many other things, and no one would probably notice that I'm gone. But it was so much more than that, Jacq. You helped introduce me to the new world of arts and entertainment through binge-watching shows and movies I have never heard of. Through that, I learned more about who you are as a person, and I loved it. That quirky side of you, that romantic-at-heart feminist who was funny and full of youthful vibrancy. As much as I made fun of those films, I found it fascinating and endearing that so many seemingly opposing aspects could exist in one person.

You were so different from me in that hopeless romantic way, Jacq, and you made me reconsider my stance on hopeless romance. You broadened my understanding of femininity by exposing my internalized negative bias. I used to think extra femininity was a weakness. That it was shallow. Perhaps that is why I was all too eager to embrace my

120

masculine, tomboyish side since my childhood. It protected me and allowed me to navigate the world with strength and authority, to be taken seriously. And honestly, it fits me like a glove. I love my gender nonconformity. I wasn't meant to be soft and gentle. But with my internalized bias against femininity, I took it as an all-or-nothing scenario, that I had to be always strong, that indulging in the whimsy and gentleness was only reserved for chick flicks and fairy tales. I knew deep down that a part of my gender expression was missing. Sometimes, I would long for the fantastical feminine feelings I saw in those movies. But I would feel ashamed of even considering it. But being with you showed me that I could be both. Years later, I would find and embrace a term that described my fluid expression: androgyny.

So maybe those chick flicks and rom-coms weren't cheesy after all, because at the heart of it was pure kindness and hope in humankind to love and be loved. I loved being invited into that space where I could also belong. This show was my attempt to introduce you to another side of me. To show you my cultural identity through performance art. I thought you would have loved it. I thought you would have loved me.

After the show, my friends, floor mates, club mates, and even folks from the Black Student Group stopped by to congratulate me. I recently made a group of new friends, and they even came to the show and congratulated me. It was a great feeling, especially since my parents and sister could not make it. But, of course, they showered me with compliments via text and phone calls. More than one. I usually shrug off compliments because I don't like drawing attention to myself and thought I was just doing my job like anyone else in my position. But this event felt different. I was so proud of what I accomplished, and I was happy other people enjoyed it. I also was looking forward to the after party that night. Another chance for us as a cast to celebrate and shake off all that stress from hard work well done.

After I ran back to the dorm to get changed for the after party, I ran into Ethan in the hallway on the way out. He smiled again. This was the tenth time he congratulated me, but the first time between just the two of us.

"I'm so happy for you! You did a great job. You look nice."

"Thank you. I really appreciate it. I'm excited to head to this party."

"Yeah, enjoy yourself. You deserve it." He lightly tapped me on the shoulder. Then he gently rubbed the side of my arm.

Wow, I thought. *This feels nice.* Even though I was getting more used to being close to people and even hugging people at times, this type of touch was rare for me to experience.

"Oh wow, you have soft skin." He said gently. I guess this was the first time he touched my arm like that. He noticed it too.

"Yeah, I guess I do." I got nervous and shivered for a slight second. I recollected myself quickly. "Must be that cocoa butter."

He laughed.

I hated myself for having that moment, enjoying that sense of touch from a friend, a male friend with a girlfriend. It was a beautiful moment, but I felt an overcast of guilt. I was so starved of physical touch that I lit up unexpectedly. Usually, I don't do that. Most times if someone brushed against me or touched my arm or shoulder, I would flinch to fight. Just ask one of my grad school peers who I unintentionally karate chopped after they caressed my shoulder in caring concern one day in class. I'm sorry about it, K. I really am. And I don't think it's linked to gender, either. I have karate-chopped many folks of different genders over the years. This was a special moment. A closer type of friend connection, but not

122

necessarily a sexual one. It wasn't a pass at me. It was a meaningful moment that sat in the between. So why is there shame around it?

Chapter Fifteen // A Quasi-Relationship Clusterfluck

After the cast party of my successful Latin American theatrical production, where I danced my feelings away to the beat of the lovely and distracting music, I experienced a hard crash back home. Those thoughts and feelings that I ignored came flying back with thrice the force. Why was I so fixated on Ethan's touch on my arm? It was so brief. Why did that sensation linger with me? I needed to sleep. I was exhausted from everything else, so these annoying thoughts were not helpful. But I couldn't sleep well that night, not really. When I finally fell asleep, I was again back in that same dream, lying in bed with Ethan, with his arms wrapped around me.

"What the hell are we going to do?" I asked calmly but solemnly, staring gently into his eyes.

"I don't know," he responded quietly.

The sound of my alarm jolted me awake. I threw my arms in the air in quiet yet frantic desperation. My arms dropped suddenly, my head and heart felt dizzy. Off to another day.

All of a sudden, I started to have cringe-attacks of moments in the past in which I began to notice some of the signs of a deep context that I was so unaware of. They flashed into my mind, having a new, clearer meaning. Ah yes, like the one time Robert wanted my pussy. Sort of. I thought it was playful banter, kind of. Let's rewind the tape.

One lovely night, the guys were getting drunk, as men do. Nope, not all men. I was not drinking. My parents ruined it for me with their Caribbean guilt trip. But I wasn't a complete nerd. I still liked hanging around with them. Drunk people are hilarious. And now that I think of it, that night was no different.

How did we get around to talking about my pussy anyway? I forget. I told you I like to joke around with vulgar sexual stuff, and we were chatting about it as usual until things took an interesting turn. Toward me. It wasn't the first time I became the focus of a sexual conversation; however, I was always the one who brought myself into it. I liked to make jokes about myself, for example, feigning interest in getting a stripper pole for the common room so I could show people my tricks. Or one time, when the boys were talking about taking showers, I jokingly asked to watch them or join in. Outrageous suggestions like that. Obviously, I would never truly do those things, and most people understood that I was trying to make those comments for their shock value. I only did it with close friends, too, who knew it was a bit.

During that one night, the jokes slowly yet suddenly turned into non-jokes. It was blurred between jokes and flirting. Robert started getting more joyful and specific with his banter. He was a happy drunk and began expressing his love and adoration toward everyone in the room... Then he turned to me.

"Hi, Pia. I'm so happy. You make me so happy."

"Yeah, I have that effect on people."

"I feel so good tonight. I'm going to sleep well tonight. Can't wait to just snuggle in my bed."

"Haha, sounds good! Maybe I should join you. Cuddle, and we can have a good night's sleep."

"Yup, that sounds great! That would make me happy."

Right then, Ethan, who was not saying much, started to perk his head up a bit. I barely noticed out of the corner of my eye, even though he was sitting next to me on the couch, and Robert was sitting on the carpet in front of us. Ethan then turned his head toward me and gave me a look, which until this day, I have no clue what it truly meant. All I knew was that it was not a positive emotion. I remember being so confused because I did not know what it meant. We were just talking; no big deal. And Robert was so drunk, he wasn't making any sense to me.

"But what about you?" Robert asked. "What would make you happy?"

This question took me by surprise. It sounded sincere and playfully existential if there ever was a case. "I don't know," I responded.

"Well, I want you to be happy. *Feel good.*"

"Okay."

"I want to make YOU feel good. Down there." Robert added.

Ethan was giving me another look.

"Wait," I paused for a second. Then I asked plainly, making sure I understood him correctly. "Do you want to eat me out?"

"*Yeah,*" Robert said, smiling.

My inner world paused for what felt like minutes. I was confused and felt a bit detached, yet filled with curiosity. This was the first time someone had offered to eat me out. It's hard to express what I felt at that moment. It was like someone was offering me something from a menu that I didn't even know was an option.

Now let me disclose my thoughts about receiving oral before I revisit my response. To put it lightly, I did not like the idea of me giving or receiving. I use those action terms because they most accurately describe my opinions about oral sex, well, at least up until two months prior to this conversation. I was mad at the idea of having to give head, mainly because all the times I heard and learned about it was in the context of necessity, of obligation. Girls were supposed to give head if they wanted to keep their men. Nope, I was not going to subscribe to that oppressive mess. Also, until then, I had never heard anyone saying that they enjoyed the act of fellatio. It sounded like an unsexy chore. No, thank you.

What about cunnilingus, you ask? Well, I felt just as disconnected and disgusted by that act as I did about fellatio. It did not sound pleasurable to me, well, up until two months before our conversation. I was beyond fortunate enough to take a class on female sexuality that made me reconsider my thoughts on oral sex. One day during class, we began talking about oral sex, and the women in the class had some very interesting positive opinions about cunnilingus. They described the experience as immensely pleasurable and something that they all wished people were more comfortable talking about. We all discussed how fellatio gets more publicity in social circles than cunnilingus and how unfair that was. Equal opportunity for pleasure became the theme of that class session. I was enjoying myself. Um, I mean the class discussion. Then someone said something about giving oral that blew my mind. I still think about it today. She said that one of the best things she likes about her sexual relationships is the ability for her to give someone else pleasure, especially oral sex. Engaging in an act that can make someone happy, in turn, made her happy and brought her and her partner closer together. In addition, it was pleasurable for her to do so. Wow, I had never thought of it that way. The way she described the act was selfless and selfish, reciprocal and non-competitive. Her words and sentiment immediately changed the way I viewed oral sex and pleasure. I could imagine myself wanting to give someone oral if they made me happy, and I could make them happy as well. Plus, it felt like a hot power move. Like, "look at me and how I made that boy cum! I'm amazing." It's the selfish part that jived with me.

Back to Robert's offer. Ah, look at the lovely predicament I was in. Notice that I only mentioned how it would feel to give someone oral? I had never thought about what it would be like for someone to want to make me feel happy in the same way. Now, calm down, low self-esteem police. No charges should be made here. I was never really sex-repulsed, but I was oral sex-repulsed for a long time. One reason was that I had never heard it described in unanimously pleasurable terms before that class, and another more significant part was that I just did not have the desire for it at all. Physically or sexually.

That is until Robert offered it to me that night. I was registering things a little differently than before in my slow-processing mind. Something that usually was not appealing to me at all started to sound slightly more appealing. Then even a little bit more appealing. I came to a realization through the way Robert was talking to me in those moments. This is someone who knew me well. And I initially became intrigued when he kept asking me what made me happy. He was being sincere, and I know this because he had also been there with me when I wasn't feeling so happy. That's what shocked me a bit when he started talking about my happiness. It was as if he was making a point to acknowledge how he had been seeing me lately. I didn't realize my friends could notice when I was truly sad. I was no longer constantly depressed like before college but I still had my depressive spouts. You know, with school and grades and growing into an adult. The usual stuff. I was feeling better that night, but when Robert brought my mood up, it made me feel seen. And when he offered to make me happy by giving me pleasure, well, it hit the spot in my heart. I know, not the first place you would think, right? Naughty people…I love ya. I felt I connected with him, and at the same time, I started to feel connected with my body. I

128

started to desire that type of pleasure. Wow, what a good, generous friend!

Y'all, y'all, I was *this* close. I was so close to saying hell yeah when I realized we were not alone in this conversation. Ethan and Joaquin were still in the room; you know from the beginning when they were always there? Face palm. It wasn't that I was afraid of being seen as a hoe, as much as my wanting to keep things secret for privacy. We were all friends, and I did not want our one night to ruin the friendship dynamic of the group. I didn't want to face the awkwardness and have to explain our encounter or the status of our relationship, especially since I did not know how I felt about Robert at the time. He still felt like a friend to me, and being forced to DTR for group harmony felt oppressive. I also thought that it would be a one-night thing the way he brought it up.

So, I took a deep breath and reluctantly declined his offer. I thought I was making the mature, right decision for our group and us and that he would understand it. It wasn't until much later that I realized that I rejected him in front of his friends and he lost face. But then again, why did he ask me in front of all of them? If he had asked me privately, I would have absolutely said yes.

I barely got the words out before Ethan quickly said to Robert, "Okay, that's enough. You're *really* drunk. Maybe we should get you to your room." *Why did he end things so abruptly*? Then I thought about the look he had given me moments earlier. I still had no clue what it meant. Why was he feeling negatively toward me? Why would he care what Robert and I did? He had a girlfriend. Ethan, not Robert. He and his high school sweetheart broke up a few months prior. And it didn't seem like his conquest for my ass was serious. No way. I almost couldn't bring myself to ponder it. Maybe it was jealousy. Nope, no way. And that would mean that Robert was really into me. Okay, that would mean two dudes in my group had a thing for me? I couldn't even imagine it.

Well, several weeks after that crazy night when nothing happened, Robert started seeing someone new. Ugh, speaking of pick-me, she was a pick-me on superspeed. Among so many different factors, I hated how she completely ignored my existence while courting Robert. It wasn't until they were official that she started to talk to me. Oh, excuse me, did you not see me there while you were laser-focused on Robert, giggling maniacally while trying to tickle him and caress his leg? Oh, and how could I forget the creepy texts? She would steal his phone, pretend to be him, and write flirty messages to all the girls in his address book just to see how they would respond. Red flag. I'm pretty sure I responded with a "Fuck off, Tiffany."

I do not want to entirely recall this other tale, so I'll just pass through it. What I did not appreciate about this pursuer was how she made me feel invisible and undesirable during her conquest. We would all hang together as a group, and she would only focus on him and everyone else who was already in a relationship. It took me a while to notice the delineation, and I was pissed when I found out. It became really evident when I was studying in the common room and she burst into it, only to engage in such outrageously obvious flirting and touchy-feely crap that I just had to leave the room. I thought I was encroaching on their space and time until after I left and realized that I was the one being encroached on. She didn't act that way around other people. The only way I can describe the act is akin to staking one's territory, and I just about had it. Well, I think we all had enough of the White woman pick-me passive-aggressive adventures for one book. One is too much, and so are they.

Maybe I was being highly attuned, or maybe there were telltale signs that I didn't notice before, but the conversations I had since the night of my final theatre production seemed to be hazed with a deeper, underlying meaning. One day after classes, Ethan and I were watching *Family Feud* in the common room. Normally, there would be more people with us, but at a certain point that afternoon, it was only the two of us. *No big deal,* I thought. I was too interested in the show to notice how many people had left. Second round, double points.

"Name a state that has the most attractive women," the host said. It was not Steve Harvey. This was a few years before the master genius graced the screen with his colorful suits. *Interesting,* I thought to myself. *I know Jersey's not on that list.*

Ethan and I took turns shouting the answers we thought were on the board. We guessed New York and California. Both were among the top answers. After New York was announced, I said to Ethan, "Yeah, I knew New York was on the list. No way Jersey would make it." I chuckled.

Ethan laughed. "Okay, yeah that makes sense."

"Yeah, you see what I mean. Compared to New York and California, Jersey girls are not as hot. I'm a Jersey 6, and look at me." I chuckled at my self-deprecating joke.

"What do you mean? You're a pretty-looking person." Ethan said plainly.

WHATTT? That response took me by surprise. He was complimenting my looks? He didn't do it out of obligation, either. Not in a "boy, I gotta say something, or she'll kill me" type of way, but genuinely, like stating an obvious fact about me. *Why?*

"Oh, really? You think so?"

He nodded.

"Well, thanks," I said sheepishly.

Where did that come from? Then I realized something. All this time, I was only thinking about my feelings. I never really gave serious thought as to how he felt about me. I assumed that my feelings were one-sided, but now I wasn't so sure. I started to ask myself the question I was too afraid to consider. The question swung between my unconscious and subconscious, stuck between my whispering id, which was my inner desires, and my overactive superego, the moral compass that would not shut the fuck up. I didn't want to go that route. The worst-case scenario would be everyone finding out how I felt and Ethan would have no choice but to reject me because there was no way he thought of me as other than a friend. But what if he didn't? What if he has other types of feelings for me? I never deeply considered it.

Then I began to run the tape back in my mind. *Were there clues that I missed this whole time?* I thought back to that night when he touched my arm. Did I forget how he recoiled slightly after touching me? As if he was surprised and embarrassed about touching me or how he felt afterward? Maybe he felt something deeper too, and he stopped himself. Was that why I felt so confused that night? That I had a lingering sensation in my heart and mind? He was complimenting me about my play, but maybe there was something more. I kept thinking that I had a moment when maybe we had a moment, and it scared us.

Something about how he gave me that compliment just now sounded... *different*. Deep down somewhere, even though I was uncomfortable, I felt that there was some truth to this. *Alright, let's get to analyzing.* In our interactions together, he seemed attentive to both Jacq and me. No big deal. It would make sense if he considered me to be a friend.

Ugh, here come the cringe moments. A little while back on the couch, Ethan was in particularly high spirits, and he plopped in between Jacq and me and put his arms around the both of us as he greeted us. I was slightly confused but open to it. Jacq did NOT look pleased. Whatever side look she gave Ethan, it was enough for him to unwrap his arms real quick. It was almost comical. But why was Jacq so annoyed when he did that? Didn't he have the right to do that based on our relationship?

Now that I think about it, why did Jacq appear uncomfortable and low-key upset this whole time? I had to think about it for a bit. Then it clicked: if her passive aggressiveness was due to low-key jealousy, then she could only be jealous if she considered me a real concern.

What? No, that could not be it. Could Jacq have considered me a... threat? That sounds so silly ! It didn't make sense to me. This wasn't a case of low self-esteem, at least for me. Then I thought about it for a while. Days, weeks. Then I finally opened up to someone about it. Not too much. I just gave the person what-if scenarios about a potential couple and a female friend, and what does it mean if the girlfriend starts acting this way around this friend...

"Yup, she's jealous," my mother said.

"*What*? No, how can you be so sure?"

"Because of everything you just said about your friend of a friend."

Sheesh, Caribbean mothers can read through anything. Well, I wasn't doing a great job of covering things. You see, until then, I didn't talk to my mother or family about my friends, let alone my situation. My mother thought I was ashamed of her, but it was almost the opposite. I wasn't ashamed of my friends, per se, but I was ashamed of myself for going through this situation. I felt ashamed that I was growing feelings for someone in a relationship and didn't want to let my family down. The main reason for going to college was to prove to myself and my family that I could succeed academically and career-wise. Friendships and relationship troubles seemed frivolous and demeaning. I didn't want to be seen as weak for dealing with this. Turns out that my family didn't think of it that way. But it would be years before I finally had the full conversation with all the juicy details to get that confirmation.

So if Jacq was jealous, and it was because she had legitimate concerns about me, why wasn't that addressed between them? *Okay, I guess it's hard for me to know about that. I don't know if they had a conversation about me.* It was hard for me to even consider them getting to the point of having a conversation about me in that sense. If they did, I assume that I would be an open productive one. White people are great at expressing their emotions, insecurities, and concerns, right? HAHAHA.

I did honestly think that way. I assumed it would have been brought up at one point since it would be hard to imagine that concern continuing to boil under the surface. Wishing this was a novel told from an omniscient point of view? Sorry, that's a no-go. Here's what I think if you'll indulge me. Maybe they did have a conversation about it, and Ethan assured Jacq there was nothing to worry about, but Jacq didn't believe him. Maybe Jacq never brought it up, out of concern for her fears being validated, or maybe she was waiting for him to bring it up, and he never did. Or maybe her passive-aggressive behavior towards us was her way of getting him to open up about it, and he never did.

Maybe he screamed my name out during a crazy bout of lovemaking, and she was like, "WHAT?" And they never spoke about it. The possibilities were endless, and if that last scenario was true, that would be HILARIOUS. It's terrible to say, but I've always had a weird fantasy of someone calling out my name while fucking someone else. Not because I want to ruin a relationship, but because it would be randomly hilarious. Are they saying it to stop themselves from coming or to MAKE themselves come? And maybe it's a compliment that they would think of me during that passionate moment. And this applies to anyone, by the way.

You're welcome.

Back to reality. I knew I had to focus. I had to look at the facts and reality of the situation. Whatever I may or may not be feeling, it had to take a backseat. I was his friend. He had a girlfriend. I was friends with Jacq. Mmh. Despite the confusing subtext and unsaid words, we did have a friendship, a good one, despite all its flaws. I genuinely enjoyed spending time with her for the most part, and she got to know and understand me in ways that many of my other peers did not. Sure, there were a lot of cons to our friendship, but it was not enough for me to throw away everything all together. Not just because of Ethan. Even if he was not in the picture, I could see us spending time together. We had a lot of interests, and I didn't forget how she made me smile and feel a broader range of emotions through art. We did get along quite well before Ethan came into the group more consistently.

That's what I reminded myself when I was conflicted with my developing feelings. Well, it was no longer developing at this point. I hated that. Imagine cruising in your car on the road of life, nothing catching your eye. Then, bam! That ornament swinging back and forth on your dashboard suddenly starts looking SO GOOD. Then all you can think of is that ornament, how shiny it looks, and how much you want to spend time with it. Over the past several months I spent with Ethan, I will admit that there were flickering moments of curiosity. But they were just that: brief moments based on the most mundane details. *Oh, I didn't realize he had dimples. Interesting. But would I want to fuck someone based on that?* No, not really. I couldn't have sex based solely on that. Or rather, I couldn't imagine having a sustained attraction based on physical attributes alone. It felt like a strained and strangely detached set of motions. As soon as I got interested, I got bored real fast.

But now, every time I was with Ethan, the emotional and physical parts connected. I wholly felt a different attraction, and it was sustained and consistent.

Then I started having more regular dreams of Ethan, and it did become a little bit easier for me to potentially fantasize about having sex with him in both my waking and sleeping states. While awake, I could get to the point where I would look at him and think about those naughty things that weren't so hard to imagine. And thinking about it was enjoyable in a more consistent way. And that horrified me. It terrified me in terms of what that meant for our relationship and his existing relationship with Jacq. Again came the guilt.

What you need to understand is that these deep feelings or an emotional attraction, now partnered with a newfound sexual attraction, took me completely by surprise. It was almost as if the—emotional connection was a prerequisite for the physical attraction to bloom, and when it did, both together, everything made sense. I began to understand what people meant by having sustained sexual attraction to people. Before, I was often confused as to how people could get sexually attracted and attached to someone in a sustained way just by looking at them. The most I would get to before was considering that I would *probably* want to hit that, but as soon as that feeling came in the past, it went away twice as fast.

Who could I talk about this with? And who would believe me? What would that sound like: "Oh yeah, this dude, I totally felt close to nothing for the longest time, now I suddenly want to jump his bones?" What was wrong with me? Deep shame. Why can't I be normal? I couldn't tell anyone about this.

I had to remind myself of the reality of the situation. Whatever this is could not be happening. I should not feel this way. I hoped that the feelings would fade away. If it took so long to develop, it might fade away fast. So I hung out with Jacq and Ethan, together and apart, as if nothing had happened. And it worked...to a point. It was uncomfortable at

136

first, but I slowly got used to it. We continued to be around each other, and I fell back into my humorous, wise-cracking self. We played games, watched television, the usual stuff. And I was still able to enjoy myself.

A mutual friend's birthday was coming up, and one day we were discussing plans. Well, the rest of the group was discussing plans. I was still salty about my birthday pity cake. Okay, I should back up for a second. I was upset about the cake Jacq gave me because of the way it was given. I'm not a self-centered person, and I usually don't like my birthdays. It always felt like it was during a time when I could never truly celebrate with peers. But when I came to college, I thought I could finally have the opportunity to share the moment with friends. I wanted it to be a low-key bonding experience. So I brought it up one day casually "I would like to do something for my birthday." They asked for the date, and I gave it to them so they knew when it was coming up.

There was a period of separation between us right before my birthday, and I was expecting someone to reach out to set up something. The last thing I heard was them saying, "yeaah, can't wait to plan something." Then crickets. No texts, emails, or phone calls. I felt uncomfortable going up and reminding them of my upcoming day, so I said nothing. I eventually thought they had forgotten. Then the day came and went. Still no phone calls, texts, emails, or FaceBook messages. Nothing. I gave up. I ran into them the following day. No open acknowledgment or greeting. *Okay, this is how we gonna play? Right...*I said nothing. Then all of a sudden, Jacq gets up slowly, almost begrudgingly, and walks away from the common room. She then enters with a sheet cake and a slight smile.

Was that for me? I was surprised. Happy Birthday, they all said. The rest of them seemed happy about it, but some of them admitted they forgot. And Jacq, the carrier of cakes, appeared flat and almost unamused. Enough for me to question if she wanted to celebrate, but not enough for me to be completely sure.

Fast forward to this situation. I was not in the mood to plan for another person's birthday. As they were planning, Jacq casually said to Ethan, "You'll probably have to remind me again as you did for Pia's birthday."

What? The? Heck? I didn't understand what was happening. So I had her clarify.

"Yeah, he told me the week before your birthday that it was coming up and we should do something about it. So we got you the cake."

OHHHHHHHHHH, you can't be serious Jacq! This can't be happening. So Ethan was the reason they remembered, and he was the reason why she got the cake. Was that why she didn't seem pleased to give it to me that day? I couldn't believe that. She was so upset he remembered and tried to do something for me that she ruined my day by gifting me in the worst way. I couldn't even get a simple recognition because she was jealous. She took that moment away from me and made it about her. The audacity. *Why did I like her again?*

But her comment made me think of something else. *Ethan remembered my birthday and tried to do something for me.* Granted, he could have done a better job of following through, especially since I was pretty sure he could see Jacq wasn't into it. He probably didn't think she would actively sabotage it, but he could have been more intentional, and I don't know, including me in the planning??? Still, learning that he was trying to do something also struck a different chord in me. I was upset, but I found it endearing of him to think of me. Oh, no. Those feelings were creeping up again.

It was like a war of emotions brewing inside of me. The constant back and forth of ambivalence was exhausting. Days turned into weeks. I didn't want to do this anymore. I didn't want to beat myself up for feeling something. I was still guilty about it, but it didn't make sense after a while to deny that I was going through *something*. It was happening, whether I liked it or not. I couldn't deny that I was regularly attracted to

138

Ethan. This attraction was not completely sexual but not exactly platonic. I wanted something closer for him and me, but sex wasn't necessarily in the equation. Most of the time, I was drawn to him and his presence. I could see myself wanting to have sex with him if that's what we both wanted to do, but I could also exist in this relationship without it. Not that sex was solely contingent on his desire or authority. It just meant that I desired a sensual connection that could exist with or without sex. This in-between realm of attachment and attraction felt foreign yet comfortable. And at a certain point, I didn't want to deny it anymore. And I also didn't want Jacq out of the picture either. I was okay with their connection if mine could also exist with him... How fucked up was that? Not really in my opinion, especially if our needs were mutually met.

I struggled internally and was losing sleep and focus. I had to do something. I wasn't ready to tell anyone how I was feeling. Truthfully, I never was. But I decided to at least acknowledge it within myself. But what was it that I was feeling exactly?

I sat in my room one night and started thinking to myself. I like Ethan. I'm attracted to Ethan. Yes, those words fit me, but something else was churning inside me, wanting to flop out of my mouth. I have feelings for Ethan. Close, but not enough. I think I... nope, no thinking. Alright, alright! What do I want to say?

I'm...in love...with Ethan. I spoke in my mind. *Say it out loud,* my conscience spoke back to me.

"I'm in love with Ethan."

Yes, that's it. It was painful to say, but there was a relief that accompanied it. From that point forward, I agreed to admit it and base my decisions and actions around that idea. *That's how I will cope,* I thought. *As long as I admit to myself. That's all I need to move forward.* The problem I later found is that

139

once you admit to loving someone, there's also an urge to tell that person how you feel, and it grows larger every day.

That's where the pain started and stayed. I was able to admit finally to myself how I felt; that it was in between sexual attraction and love that existed at the same time. Nothing, nothing, nothing, then bam! Emotional attraction, sensual attraction, and love were all thrown upon me at once. Every time I saw him, I thought, *Yup, I love this man.* While we're out eating, *Yes, I definitely love this man.* Here we are, playing video games. *I love this man. Sorry to this man, but I love him.*

Then a thought kept creeping in my mind: "You have to tell him."

No, I can't. That makes no sense.

"You need to tell him. You love him."

Why should I do that? It was as if my mind and body were propelling me to eject my feelings into the world as if to say that feelings are meant to be shared not stored.

What the hell do my mind and body know? Turns out, **everything**.

Chapter Sixteen // Self Disclosure

It's hard for me to open up to people sometimes. Okay, many times. Most of the time, it was such an innate tendency that I did not realize the choice until later. However, one of the most intentional omissions was not speaking about my friends to my parents. At first, I did not fully understand why I did not talk about my friends to my folks or, more importantly, what I was going through. That last part - what I was going through - was the source of my omission. At some significant level, I was embarrassed that I was having such difficulties within my friend group, and I did not want to burden or shame my family for not knowing what to do. When you are a first-gen student from a Latinx/Caribbean immigrant family, you experience many firsts. However, there is still this expectation that you represent your family while away. And while this mainly applied to academics and workplaces, I internalized the sentiment in my interpersonal interactions and social relationships. Even if I did not know all the social norms and rules of college life, I was still expected to behave respectfully and kindly, which honors my family's upbringing. So if I, for example, got caught sleeping with my professors solely to get good grades, those actions would bring academic troubles for sure, but it would also disgrace my family because it would tarnish my reputation and sour people's perceptions of me. In other words, families like ours view their offspring as a reflection of the family's values and upbringing. So if the child messes up or misbehaves, then it would appear to others that my folks did not raise them right, thereby disgracing the caregivers.

I was not "allowed" to be held up in seemingly frivolous romantic drama or entanglements because those situations were considered to be looked down upon in our cultures. According to their values, I was mainly there for school. While they acknowledged the importance of social/romantic life, I shouldn't be caught up in the insignificant drama, especially if it negatively impacted my grades. I would be mortified if I had to tell my parents that I failed a class due to a relationship. I probably would have to pack my bags before telling them the news, with plans of another place to live in the summer. Do White people not have to worry about that stuff? Jealous.

I took it to another level in that I also believed I should be able to handle conflict or drama on my own, or more specifically, I should know what to do and how to resolve things. And most importantly, I should not be so affected by these things, like an overwhelmed, heartbroken lead in a romantic film. It seemed weak and frail to let those feelings get to me like that. So I did not discuss those matters with my family. But there was another aspect to it: I thought the mere mention of my friends to my folks would mean that those relationships were real and, in turn, those feelings and issues were real. And I was not ready to accept that, outside of speaking the truth in my mind.

The lack of disclosure worked both ways but to a lesser extent. My friends did know general facts about my parents and my younger sister. Seeing their reactions to certain sayings, I would have about my folks was funny. In particular, whenever my friends would mention getting away with something with their parents, I would often say: "My parents would shoot me if I did that." I guess I said it too often because one day, Robert said: "Wow, you have a violent way of explaining your parents' reactions." I guess so, Robert, I guess so.

So I did talk about my family often, but if I'm honest, it was mainly surface details. Maybe I'm not giving myself credit. It was a little under the surface but not too deep. I realized my limit for sharing details when I had to deal with a health scare within my family. It was hard to learn about it and not be able to do much since I was a three-hour flight away. It wasn't a severe enough issue that I had to fly back home, but I had to deal with the uncertainty of upcoming medical tests and await the results. And worse of all, it was happening right before a planned family weekend visit. So, if things went well, it would be a great treat, but if things were not, it would dampen the visit tremendously.

I remember the night before my mother had to go to testing; the night before, she would learn her results. That second night was much more terrifying and uncomfortable for me. I tried my best to hide my nervousness the whole day while with my friends. Around nighttime, I noticed myself getting more jittery while sitting in the common room. The rest of the squad left one by one until it was just Ethan and me. Ethan stood up and was on his way out, and I sat behind. I didn't want to get up or head to bed yet because that meant the next day was closer. So I stayed, slumped on the couch. But not too slumped, for appearances' sake. Ethan said goodbye, and I vaguely heard it. I felt frozen, like everything was moving in slow motion. Thinking he left, I said to myself, "Yeah, whatever. I'll just stay here. I'm so sad." I stared at the floor for several seconds. Then I looked up and noticed Ethan was sitting in the chair diagonally in front of me.

"Are you *okay*?" He asked gently.

"What?" I snapped my posture suddenly, not expecting him to still be there. "I'm fine. Yeah. *I'm good.*"

"Are you sure?" Ethan looked at me, kind yet concerned. He wasn't leaving. *Why won't he leave?* I couldn't believe he was perceptive. I thought White folks don't pick up subtle cues like that. And now? The countless times growing up when I showed emotion to varying degrees in front of my White peers, they rarely, if barely, noticed. And now, when I don't want to be noticed, I finally get noticed?

"Yeah, I'm just tired."

"Do you want me to stay with you? Help you get to your room?"

"No, I should be fine." I started to get up.

"Thank you."

"Okay," he said. Then we walked out of the room together.

I remember that day vividly, and I often think to myself, *Why didn't I tell him what was happening with my family and me?* I guess I didn't want him to be worried or to drop something so heavy on him, especially at night. Plus, I didn't think he could do anything to help me. Or so that's what I thought before I realized he was volunteering to stay with me. I never imagined that scenario happening. Afterward, I got some sleep, and it turned out all well in the end. My mother came to see me, and I was glad to have her visit. But that also meant she would run into my friends at some point. Oh, goodness.

Caribbean parents are a trip, especially mothers. They may be caring, but they are the realest people I know. Truth over harmony was scripture to them. They will tell it to you straight and blunt, no questions asked. It was common growing up to expect the truth and nothing but the truth, regardless of how hard or painful it was to hear as a child. Yet, I internalized this way of parenting so much that I assumed it was the same for most people, including White folks. Did you know that some parents hide or sugarcoat the truth to protect their children's feelings? I sure as hell didn't, not until I was today years old. Must be nice, White folks. So when she visited, I knew my friends were going to be read the fuck out.

I admit I was a fucking coward who avoided the inevitable as long as I could. But it was a bad look on me and, in turn, a bad look on my family. Interestingly enough, I was stalling on both sides. My friends asked me when my mother was arriving as if they were anticipating and looking forward to seeing her. I

144

gave them minimal details. It got so awkward that at some point, my mother and my friends asked if I was embarrassed by them on separate occasions. That made me feel worse, especially when my mother said it. No, I wasn't embarrassed by any of them. I thought they were all great people. I was embarrassed by myself. I can't explain it, but the situation itself, the idea of everyone being in the same room with all those vibrant personalities, stressed me out. I honestly thought I would explode. I'm typically not a socially-anxious person, but this was perhaps one of the rare times in my life that I was so shakingly nervous and apprehensive that I dissociated myself from having to deal with any of those feelings that made no sense to me. The only analogy I could use would be if former First Lady Michelle Obama and, I don't know, the cast of Friends met each other. What the hell would I be doing in that situation, in the background? Like, why would I even exist in that situation? Nope, gotta run.

To answer your burning questions, yes. My mother finally got to meet my friends. Well, some of them. Jacq happened to not be there when she came. Perhaps for the best. Jacq would have been dragged for days if she had pulled any of that passive-aggressive shit in front of my mother. Black people don't mess with disrespect like that, which is what it would look like to her. She did, however, get the chance to meet Ethan. It was fine, I guess. No, seriously, it was a nice moment. They met each other and smiled. My mother paused slightly after shaking his hand, then she proceeded to scan him up and down. It was very subtle and super quick, but as a descendant, I could spot that check right away, like a half-blood or wizard witnessing a magic trick. The muggles couldn't see it, but I knew what she was up to. She gave a slight nod as if to say to me and him, "Okay, alright. I see. I approve." Approve of what, exactly? I never said anything. Do you think she saw past my thinly veiled what-if-scenario question about jealousy a while back? Too cunning. Or, more accurately, I couldn't keep a secret or hide my feelings for shit. She knew something was up, but she could not openly confirm it.

You never realize how little other people know about the nuanced parts of your Blackness until something terrible happens. Obviously, my friends knew I was Black, but I guess they didn't give as much thought to how my Black differed from other types of Black. Or I should say, how salient my Black immigrant identity was until something painful happened. I distinctly remember telling people about my specific ethnicity. On several occasions.

They had to know where my family came from and the country where my parents were raised. But somehow, on that day and the painful week that followed, I resorted to questioning myself if I ever did give that information. No, I must have. I didn't talk about it every minute of every day, but I mentioned it from time to time. Or did I? I wasn't ashamed of it. Oh, no, my second-gen guilt was creeping up again, where your parents conditioned you to think that you were ashamed of the culture if you didn't talk about it enough. Oh, goodness. *Did I subconsciously mask my family's culture in front of my college peers? No, that can't be it.* But why didn't anyone call or text me that night? Did they not see the news? It was on every local and national channel, constantly updating. CNN, ABC, NBC, FOX. All the channels.

I was overthinking this. Yes, I was. I began to remember some of the times I mentioned my Caribbean culture. Even made jokes about how our cake was the best type of cake there was. None of this American store-bought dry cake nonsense. You can imagine why I was extra mad about the birthday cake fiasco, but I digress. Even Robert and I made a fake promise that I would teach him how to make it for his family at Christmas. I wished I could, but my ass cannot bake for shit.

I happened to be home with my family when we got the news. An earthquake. A massive one that left devastation and disaster. We were a few hours' flight away, yet too far to do anything. I was nervous and in disbelief. The news was coming in incomplete pieces, being updated with vague details. And then came the pictures. Fun fact, The Associated Press was the first company to release images from the ground. I didn't know who they were before then, but ever since that night, I get flashbacks to that day when I first learned their name every time I see a post or article from them. The ground ruptured into pieces, rubble scattered all around. Grey, black tar everywhere. There was something else, but I couldn't make it out from a distance. I leaned in closer. There they were. Bodies, crushed in between the rubble, almost indistinguishable. I turned my head.

Little did I know that those photos would be the first of hundreds on display through sensationalized media. Pictures of poor Black folks in despair, bleeding, crying, broken. Images that made me cringe and die inside, with no room for tears. Later those images would signify different meanings. For folks of my culture and similar, it would be a reminder of the dangers and horrible impact of global warming. It would be a reminder of the devastation wrought through colonization. We should have been able to withstand this natural disaster, but we did not have the resources or infrastructure to protect us. We would have if it weren't for the fucked up history of American and European forces enslaving us, murdering us, and literally making us pay for our freedom. Because they did not see us as real people, as independent people capable of taking care of ourselves. And they made damn sure over the past couple of centuries to prevent us from becoming as prosperous as we were when we were enslaved by them, and they reaped profits for our natural resources, our food, our land. The land that at that moment was once again damaged, this time by nature itself. For folks outside our culture, mainly White folks, it was sensationalized trauma porn: a way for them to get a glimpse of our pain and suffering, but not fully understand. America and Europe have a funny type of amnesia. The one where they conveniently forget that they are part of the reason we were currently impoverished, ripe for the picking from this disaster. We should have been able to weather this disaster, but the echoes of history took that away from us.

I am glad I was with my family when I first saw and heard about the devastation from the earthquake.

We were at home, but we were constantly moving around: us listening to the radio, my parents calling and texting other family members, and me just pacing aimlessly in and out of my parents' bedroom, where the TV was on throughout the night. At a certain point, one of my parents asked me about my phone. They wanted to know how many friends were checking in on me that night. Their phone was constantly ringing and binging; surely they thought mine was too.

But my phone was silent. Not silent mode, just not making any noise because no one was calling me. No one was texting me. What? My parents were confused. Surely my friends knew what was going on, they thought. It was on every TV channel; it had to be trending on social media. I didn't have the internet on my phone, so I wasn't getting updates on Facebook. And I didn't check my laptop. Not that it would matter because I got no DMs and no posts on my wall. But my friends could text me. Still, silence.

"What is wrong with your friends?" my parents asked. "Clearly, they know where you're from? Right, Pia?"

"I think so," I said. My head dropped, slightly confused. I was ashamed. I didn't want my parents to think I purposely withheld that information from them.

They did know, right? I asked myself. *Remember, that joke they made about making a cake from our home country for Christmas? Yes, Pia, yes.* I was sure. Almost sure. Maybe sure. *They had to know, right? It's an important part of my identity. I didn't wear flags and traditional garb, whatever that meant, but I didn't have to do that, right? Remember, Pia? Remember that time we played Catchphrase, and you gave that clue to Jacq, the one where you said, "the country next to the country where I'm from? And she got it immediately? If you knew the country next to my country, she had to know my country, right? What kind of fucked up rabbit hole of thinking is this?*

I snapped myself out of it. I eventually went to bed sometime at night. I thanked the heavens that I had a late afternoon flight the next day because I needed to sleep. I woke up the next day to no messages, voicemails, or missed calls. Silence, again. My parents shook their heads. They couldn't believe my friends did not have the decency to check in with me.

Let me back it up a second here. Throughout my life, my parents have had a pattern of telling me how friends *should* behave, and how my experiences with my peers were often far away from that. It started in elementary school, and it became the way I found out that I was being bullied and that I had toxic friends who treated me unfairly. Real friends should take an interest in you, they would say. Real friends would invite you to their house and not just expect you to only accommodate them at yours. Real friends would check in with you throughout the year, not just in school. It had been years since they made those comparisons, and I thought I had escaped the land of toxicity, especially since I started college. I completely forgot about those patterns, those wise parental sayings on friendship. Subconsciously, I thought I was in a better place. That moment made me feel like I had slid back to the beginning. And I was enraged at my so-called friends. *Yeah,* I thought. *My parents were right. How dare they not*

149

reach out to me? They weren't bullies, so what was going on here?

I am going to flip and reverse this bit here. Telling the story backward from this point will make greater significance. You can probably guess that I eventually had a conversation with my squad, but let's dive into what I learned about their initial responses many years later. Yup, that's right. After college. You see, this was my first very direct, harsh lesson in fragility and its crippling effect on action, or inaction in this case, as in most cases. I know that everyone in my squad, nay, the whole university knew what happened that weekend. It was national news, so yes, it became common knowledge. Now, Whiteness has a weird sense of amnesia. Somehow the fragility and discomfort from the news created a chasm in their minds where my identity got disconnected from the natural disaster. In other words, I believe the discomfort in knowing they had a friend who was affected by this news made them conveniently forget I was part of those affected by the news. I am not justifying their inaction because I fully acknowledge the stupidity in this logic, the cowardice, the entitlement of their feelings to mine. I also fully believe that they recognized that my home country was affected, and not knowing what to say, or should I say, not knowing the perfect response, prevented them from reaching out... Or they may have thought that someone else would reach out to me before them, and I became a victim of the bystander effect. Or maybe they did not think it was important enough of an event to reach out to me. That was the worst-case scenario for me back then and now. That they looked at the news, noted it was about me, and didn't care enough about it to check in with me. I hope that was not the real scenario. Most likely, they didn't know what to say, so they said nothing, thinking it would go away, like their discomfort. I will never understand that as a viable option: to pick inaction out of not having the perfect answer. Anything was better than nothing. Good people can do terrible things. This is where my interaction with Ethan began and ended.

Let's just say that I hopped off the plane red-hot. Before I left, I started a conversation with my family about how I would approach my so-called friends when I got back to campus. Maybe it was our need to distract ourselves with the pain, but our conversation about my approach became so over-animated and exaggerated that it was hysterical. We got hype, particularly with one of my parents, about the idea of my cussing these fools out. It was sweet justice for us. One of my parents wanted live text updates. Oh, you about to get the deets, I told her, *cough* I mean, *them*. I'm about to ROAST THESE CRACKERS! That's what I thought and texted her that night...I mean, them.

I went to the room, dropped off my baggage, and walked right into the common area. And there he was, Ethan, sitting his dumb clueless-looking ass on the couch.

"Hey," he said, happy to see me.

Oh, he got eyes, and they work since he can see me. But he's happy to see me? That's not right. "Hey!" I said, starting soft and slow but ending with a higher, emphatic tone.

"How was your vacation?" *Oh, that's it. He did it now. He went right in with that question, asking me about my vacation as if nothing had happened? He is about to get THIS right here.*

"How was my vacation? Um, let me see. Started good, you know, but then something happened toward the end. I wonder what that was," I ended sarcastically.

"Huh," he said, confused.

"Did you see the news?"

"Yeah, I guess."

151

"So you know what happened in that country this weekend?"

"Yeah," he said as if it didn't matter.

"Oh, so you did, then, and you didn't say anything? *Why didn't you call me*?"

"I don't know. I don't know."

"You don't know?"

"Well, I didn't know you were from-"

"**WHHHHAAATTT**?" I yelled.

"You didn't know I was from there, that my family was from there?" My guilt for them not knowing was masked by my flaming rage at this stupidity. I didn't realize it then, but I was rightfully mad about this. I remember being ashamed right afterward and the shame lingering for a long time. I thought it was my fault for them not knowing. I didn't understand until years later that they should have known. They did know. And if they didn't, it was their fault for not knowing or inquiring further about my cultural background. White/no culture is not the default for everybody.

"I'm sorry."

"You're *sorry*?"

"I don't know..." *What to say*, he was probably going to tell me. Ethan, someone I thought of having a sense of certainty, was silent, slumped, stuck. It infuriated me.

I shifted to the side, quickly shooting one of my parents the roasting crackers text. "Yes! You let them motherf*ckers know!" was her wonderful reply. Screw maturity; she was on my side. No fucks given.

Now, I couldn't get away with slapping a man in public, let alone a White man, but deep down, I didn't want that to happen. I didn't want any of this to happen this way. But there I stood, five feet short, towering over this six-foot man, sitting down, slumped, stuck. It was weird and shameful for me, yet hysterically ridiculous.

It was easier for me to lean into this comical rage than to deal with the underlying feelings. When I saw his inaction, his being stuck, it lit a fire of rage in my soul, but it also created a well of despair deep, flowing into my heart. There was another realm of emotions that were stirring up, ones I did not want to acknowledge, ones that I felt embarrassed and ashamed to have, especially at this sad moment in time.

Somehow, in this terrible moment, this moment of reflecting on tragedy, I felt love, attraction, and emotional attraction turning into physical temptation. I was mortified, and that fueled the rage. But this rage was shaky, not on firm ground with the authority it had at the moment. When he stood there, clearly not knowing what to say or what to do, I felt helpless. I wanted him to read my mind. I wanted him to see through the bullshit bravado I was masquerading at that moment. To see what I truly wanted him to do for me. I wanted him to hold me. To stop me from shaking, to ground me. I wanted him to look into my eyes, to truly see me and acknowledge the pain that I was feeling, and to acknowledge that he fucked up by not seeing me before. I wanted him to kiss me, either soft or hard, fast or slow. I wanted him to lift me and take me down. To rip my clothes off, the rush of that excitement masking my pain, distracting me from the despair yet acknowledging it at the same time. I wanted him to fuck me and, in that fucking, to bond with me, to take care of me, to make me feel better by showing that he cared.

I had never felt so physically attracted and disconnected at the same time. I was shocked and embarrassed by my desire to want him so deeply, someone in a relationship with someone else. But I didn't care. I wanted to be with him in that way, at that moment, for that night. I was ashamed because I sexually wanted physical intimacy during a time I was grieving. I didn't think it was normal or appropriate. And worst of all, it felt like the manufactured fake love scenes from Jacq's video vault. And it felt so demeaningly submissive. I was upset again. This was the type of anger that was a result of my needs not being met. But I knew the discrepancy between my desires and my outward behavior. How could he know I wanted to be consoled, to at least be held? I wasn't communicating any sense of wanting gentleness. And for me to ask for it? Absolutely not. I didn't think I deserved that right, even to be held. And I didn't dare risk rejection.

After I finished quickly texting my parents, I returned, but I could tell he was exhausted. The energy had shifted. More people came. Or I should say, Robert came. *Geez, I didn't have the energy to wring him out at the same high level.* But I didn't have to because Ethan filled him in. Honestly, I don't remember Robert's reaction as much as Ethan's. Maybe I was tired at that point. Maybe I was more concerned about Ethan's response than his. So sad, too, because I was still hurt by his ignoring me. Somehow the conversations had moved onward, and it was then that I found out that Ethan and Robert had plans to go to another apartment for a hang, and they had originally planned to invite me along.

"But I guess you wouldn't be in the mood to go out tonight." He assumed.

"Nope. I want to go with you," I said firmly. I wasn't going to stay home alone that night. And it looked like they were going to go with or without me, and I was NOT going to make it easy for them. Them leaving me and getting away with that? Good people do terrible things. I wanted them to see me, to know I was still there. I did not care if they were uncomfortable. Little did I know how much I enjoyed that discomfort.

We went over to a mutual friend's apartment for a simple chill hang. Soft music was on in the background, and people were standing around talking while others were playing beer pong. Fuck that game. It haunted me wherever I went. But I let it slide into the background of my pain that night. We eventually sat down and started talking to some new people. We bonded over our interest in a long-running show at that time. A situational comedy about finding one's married partner, the mother of the lead's children. You know the one. I got into the conversation. It was a show that I liked and felt comfortable talking about it. It was a good distraction from the hell that was the night and evening before. Ethan was into it, looking at me and turning his head to nod at the person speaking. It was a subtle gesture, but I took note in the back of my mind. Ethan was into it, almost too into the conversation. Or was he too into me and how I was into the conversation?

Ethan was, of course, drinking that night. That wasn't remarkably strange, but it seemed a little different. I couldn't put my finger on it. He was…talkative, but not too much. He sounded slightly nervous in his speech. He was saying more words in sentences at a given moment, but not too many words. He was tipsy but not drunk. His speech was not slurred. He was…talkative. I did not make the connection between the pain he thought he caused me and his drinking to deal with it. I didn't think I had that effect on someone. I didn't think someone would care to be fucked up in public like that.

Then it clicked for about two seconds in my mind before I second-guessed myself and shook it off. The multiple subtle looks at me were his attempt to check in with me that night to make sure I was okay. He was trying to make sure I wasn't uncomfortable or sad, but I didn't make it easy for him, being hard to read. I guess he knew me well enough to realize I tend to mask my feelings in public, but I also was not the one to hide or outwardly lie about going through something. I didn't tell anyone at the party about what was happening back home for me. Slowly through the night, I did start talking more. I faintly remembered later that night that Ethan did explicitly ask me if I was okay. I didn't think much of it, since it was a normal thing to ask of anyone. *"You good?"* Nothing to it. Well, so Ethan wasn't a Black man with swagger, so he didn't say it as smoothly as that, more of a *"You okay?"* Still, it became more apparent later on that he felt bad about what happened that evening in his weird, subtle way (which was probably not at all subtle to him, but definitely to me). Really bad. To the point that he drank to cover his feelings and became publicly intoxicated. Not that I noticed since I, too, was in much pain and it blurred my alright terrible radar for subtleties. He didn't know what else to say or do besides those subtleties, which were no substitute for the pain that he caused by his inaction. And he knew that. Good people do terrible things.

And where was Jacq? She was not back on campus that night, coming home the next day. By the time she came back, I was over it. I believed she was the one who mentioned it to me first, probably after someone told her I was upset. "Beware of the monster that lies in waiting for you," they probably said. I may be paraphrasing here, who knows? I didn't yell at her because I knew her passive aggressiveness would not respond to my directness. Plus, it had failed with Ethan, so I didn't bother to do it again. She did acknowledge what happened and, in doing so, took some accountability. The moment she saw me, she addressed the elephant in the room. I felt conflicted because I was past giving people the benefit of the doubt. It worked in my favor to stay mad at her. It felt justified, like another tangible reason to prove she didn't like me.

But obviously, I wanted her to care, or else I wouldn't have been so hurt by her inaction as much as Ethan's. She could have used this situation to be passive-aggressive again, but even she realized that would be too cruel. Perhaps I wanted her to slip into her old ways, so it would justify my desire for Ethan that night. *See, he is the only one who cared for me,* I thought. But she didn't, and that made me uncomfortable. She was kind, even though she did not openly have conversations about how everything was affecting me. Perhaps she, like the other White people in my life, did not know how to hold that type of space for me. *What would that look like for them? To be so comfortable and secure in themselves to sit there and let me release all my anger and emotions about that whole disaster and not take it personally.* That's what I needed: someone to give me that space to openly say and feel whatever I was feeling without them being defensive. But I didn't know how to articulate that at the time, nor did I think I needed to, and they did not have the insight to know it was an option. So all Jacq could do was acknowledge that it happened and talk about it when it came up on the news, in class, and on campus. I still struggle with feeling it was enough to believe they all made up for their initial inaction.

I think they all donated to charities, but I'm not sure. I want to believe that. As for my school? Well, they raised a shit-ton of money. Like, more than I thought and gave it more attention than I thought. Wow, I had never seen as many White people knowingly volunteer at the drop of a hat to fly to a third-world country to help out in a disaster. Well, America was part of why it is a third-world country, so I guess it was the least they could do, but I digress. The only time I got upset was while Robert and I were passing by one of their fundraising tables. They asked us if we wanted to donate. It shook me, and I dissociated. I typically get nervous about giving donations, often thinking I never have enough money to give. And in this situation, donating made the crisis so much more real. And I wanted to empty all my pockets, to give up all my savings, and it still wouldn't be enough. Robert noticed my hesitance and perhaps my underlying sadness, which I didn't realize he noticed, and he politely declined for the both of us.

As we were walking, the White male student at the table said something like us not caring about the people or the cause... The audacity of this asshole. *How dare he?* I feel like

157

it was a stupid bet to assume that whoever he was talking to would not be part of the culture for which he was fundraising. Oh, I wanted to walk up, cuss him out, and knock the shit out of him. Listen, I feel like I need to make a point about my aggression and say I did not hit him. As a Black woman, I can't be seen as angry or aggressive. And if I think of aggressive stuff, I am not a real, fully evolved person. But fuck it, don't we all have those thoughts? So many times, people have said some shit to me, and the first thing I think to do is put these hands on them. Every adult person has done this. Terrible thoughts make up good people…sometimes.

Eventually, my squad got to a point where they could be in the same space with me and hear me complain about the awful things happening in my country. Not necessarily my feelings of despair but anger about the injustice. Media proved helpful in disarming some of that tension in the room. In addition to our TV shows and rom-coms, we also got into the habit of watching late-night news, well, the comedic version of late-night news. It allowed us to keep up with the country, through irreverent and poignant social commentary. So when those shows started covering that content, it became easier for me to comment on it. I remember one story of how White Americans were trying to rescue children in my country who were kidnapped, only to learn that the children were not in danger and the White folks were the kidnappers by taking those children away. Classic ignorance and White saviorism. We could all acknowledge and criticize that for what it was. I could talk about it again with Jacq when it appeared on the Disney Channel. I was shocked when I first saw the commercial of Disney stars talking about their experiences of hearing the news about my country. It was the first time I saw Disney tackle a hard subject on their channel. Jacq and I talked about the importance of it. I was glad they were open to discussing the impact on children. I felt seen, and hoped the kids from my country watching the channel felt the same.

Even though it became a bit easier to talk about the aftermath of the natural disaster, it was still all on a surface level. I never truly opened up about my feelings. It was mainly an automatic response, one brought out of self-preservation. I never considered going there, especially when it came to crying. First of all, I've always had an issue with crying. Believe it or not, I could relate to Cameron Diaz's character from *The Holiday*, as we both struggled to cry. They jokingly called it neck spasms in the movie when she felt the urge to cry, but nothing came out. My tear ducts never developed the ability to burst in full streams, particularly with the accompaniment of audible sounds. It seemed too dramatic and distant from my sense of being. This is going to sound strange and awful, but as much as I hate the concept of White tears and how they shut everything down in public, I've always been a bit jealous of White women's ability to cry so fully at an instant moment. Granted, White tears are a manipulative tactic to escape accountability, but I did relish the idea of enjoying the release of emotion in public nonetheless. My tear ducts were permanently clogged and would only occasionally leak in private. One of the many aspects I liked about Jacq was that she never engaged in that tearful bullshit. I appreciated that about her, whether I realized it or not. I never had to worry about her crying or becoming whiny to turn the attention to her. If anything, I think we made fun of folks who did that. As I mentioned before, she is not a Karen. I didn't fuck with people like that. Maybe we did have more in common than I thought: we both appeared to be tougher than the average woman, very open-minded, and never super emotional. Well, Jacq was a little bit more feminine than I, outside of the emotional part. Maybe that is what I loved and found intriguing about her. She had that masculinity in her boldness yet she still openly loved undeniably feminine things like Disney. And the intersection of that, along with Disney now discussing this deeply painful topic, gave us a chance to bond, albeit just a little bit. But never too down the road of emotions.

I never considered communicating my need to my squad of space to talk about my pain with the potential of bursting into tears. That release would have been what I needed, but I was unaware of my desires at that moment. I also could not imagine them taking me up on my offer. If the thought did cross my mind, I would immediately dismiss it. I thought they would never want me to do that, and at the same time, I assumed they knew what I needed and didn't care. It didn't cross my mind until years later that I never really gave them a chance. It was a complex issue. As a Black woman, I never wanted to cry in public out of concern of being seen as weak. I also thought my emotions were not as valued or respected as other folks. Being angry in public? Yes, that was a win for me. Anger had power and authority; it commanded attention and respect. It produced fear in others, which at that time, I capitalized on due to wanting others to share my pain. If they couldn't feel the same pain I was feeling, at least they could feel the fear from how much I was going through. That belief was the catalyst for my fight with Ethan, which I believe was not a fight but a productive conversation.

On the other hand, I believed that not seeing Jacq openly cry or express vulnerable emotions in public fueled my illogic to further conceal mine. If this White woman wasn't doing it around us, why the hell would I go down that road? But I wonder now: what would it have been like to give myself that space? I believe it's the same justification for why I didn't drink in college. I did not trust other people to take care of me if I became intoxicated. I thought they would leave me to rot, to fall prey to predators who would take advantage of me. I consciously and intentionally made the decision not to drink for those reasons, but I guess I also subconsciously made the decision not to be emotionally vulnerable for just the same. I think it was a disservice to the friendship not to trust them. Perhaps Jacq would put a cork on her passive-aggressive side and would have softened her demeanor if she saw me truly in pain. It makes sense now; I doubt she would have capitalized on that situation. It had nothing to do with Ethan, and she wasn't a fucking monster. But I never gave her a chance. And she was never openly vulnerable enough around me to give that space. Good people can do ignorant things.

Throughout my academics, I was able to hone my interests and explore the field of psychology and other related fields. I got interested in the gender and sexuality courses and was particularly invested in a course where we did a study on casual sexual relationships. See? I was fascinated by sex, even if it wasn't directed towards me. Anyway, my classmates and I had to split into groups based on an area of interest within this broad topic. We determined the areas of interest by listing categories, most of which were demographic populations.

"Freshmen experiences!" someone shouted.

Added to the board.

"LGBTQ+," someone else said.

Added to the board.

"Age differences!" Okay. I wasn't sure how broad of an age range we hoped to get in a college setting, but it didn't matter because it was added to the board.

I felt like I had to contribute something to the conversation. "Experiences in the Black community!" I shouted. People nodded and smiled in agreement. It looked like there was interest in that topic, just like the others. *Added to the board*.

Alright, that day was done. I felt happy about my participation, and I was looking forward to the next session, where we got to pick our groups. Can I tell you all a secret? Even though I added the topic to the list, the Black experience group was not my first choice. I know. I'm a bad Black person.

Shame onto the culture. In all seriousness, I wanted to be part of the Freshman group. I was very interested in learning more about how folks who just started college thought about and approached sexuality and casual sex relationships. In the back of my mind, I always assumed I would also consider race as a factor within that group. I assumed it would be an inherent factor within all the groups.

The next session arrived, and I sat in quiet anticipation. The professor wrote the groups in sections across the board. The freshman group was first. Several people quickly raised their hands. They were all chosen in front of me. *Shoot!* I wasn't quick enough. The LGBTQ+ group was next. I didn't raise my hand. It looked like everyone knew who already wanted to be part of that group beforehand. If I had to pick a second choice, I wanted to be part of the Black experience group over the LGBTQ+ group. I thought I didn't know enough about the LGBTQ+ community to volunteer as a researcher (a sentiment that has changed significantly for the better years later, but I digress…). Soon enough, the Black experience was placed on the docket. I shot up my hand fast, thinking I would have to fight the rest of the folks for a spot. No one else raised their hands. I was the only one. I was mortified and confused. Where was all the interest from earlier in the week? I scanned the room and saw the awkward, uncomfortable glances of those peers who were initially so excited. Since there were no other volunteers, the group was crossed from the list. I ended up in the age differences group.

"What *happened*?" I asked the class openly during the next session the following week. "I thought folks were interested in that group."After what felt like hours of silence, some students spoke up. "I wasn't sure if I could be part of that group. I thought it would be awkward as a White person to study Black students. I thought it would be weird for me to go up to them on campus and ask questions." Other students nodded in agreement.

I should clarify. As you probably already knew, the class was overwhelmingly White. One other Black person in the course had articulated his strong interest in joining the LGBTQ+ group from the beginning. That made sense to me. Once again, just because we're Black didn't mean we had to join the Black experience group. But what about the rest of them? I was confused by their responses, but I let it go. My professor was the only one who spoke to me after class and apologized for their behavior. She was ashamed of what she called "a typical White student response" at our college. I was a little embarrassed that I did not understand what she meant then. I understand it all too well, but back then, that was my first major experience of White fragility and discomfort.

Needless to say, I was disappointed that the Black Experiences group was erased from our project. I went home and ran into Ethan and some other female friends that night. We were on our way out for the night when I brought up the class situation in the car. Everyone shook their heads in disappointment, and disbelief, because of course.

"I'm sorry you had to go through that," Ethan said.

"Yeah, me too."

It was a simple comment, but it showed support because he did not question me or try to provide an excuse for my peers' behavior. Truth be told, this is a basic requirement of support. At a minimum, this is what I expected as a response from a White person. Little did I realize that this type of response was rare, and most other times I experienced some type of White discomfort and fragility in public settings. In the years since then, the responses I got have been overwhelmingly defensive, or should I say, in defense of Whiteness. So, yes, I am glad that Ethan responded this way, but also, that is what a friend should do. So I didn't congratulate him or anything, and it didn't seem like he was looking for that. Once again, what you would expect from a friend.

So why do I bring this up? An example of basic kindness and support of a friend. Well, I also noticed this was one of the rare moments I openly talked about race. That was a problem, not feeling comfortable enough to process such micro-aggressions with my White friends. *Just say friends*, Pia. You know you didn't hang out with Black folks in college. Okay, that's an exaggeration. I did spend time with Black people, just not as often. It would be for special occasions, like parties and cultural events. But yes, on the reg, I would hang with the Whites. From the sidelines, I did see how close my Black peers were with one another. They were a tight group, and I am specifically talking about the folks within my cohort. I don't remember how I got this statistic, but I learned early on that there were 91 of us. And they looked like rock stars to me. Black pride and excellence all the time. They were so creative and excellent that they claimed a specific table within one of the dining halls as their spot. I'm talking about a large dining hall and visiting center for the whole campus. They found a large round table in the middle and were like, "Yup, we claiming this one." That's it. No questions asked. Who knew that years later, this idea for a place where Black folk can gravitate toward one another would be the genesis of a multimillion-dollar social media news company? My peers capitalized on that theme of community to basically create Black Buzzfeed. I'm not jealous at all. What did I tell you? *Black excellence*.

Day after day, whenever I passed through that building's ground floor during lunchtime, you best believe they were chillin' and having the best damn time. I never sat at the table. Part of it was due to a lack of interest, which sounds terrible. It took me a long time to get used to eating in front of my close friends, and I wasn't looking to expand my group for lunchtime. Wait, did I graze again by a potential eating and body image issue? *Yup*, and I'll do it again.

One faithful day came when I was once again passing by the cafeteria on the ground floor. I was expecting to see the usual Black crew when out of the corner of my eye, I saw a White person at the table. Okay, not a big deal. Every once in a while, a White person or two would hang with the crew... They weren't against White people being at the table as long as they knew they were hanging at the Black table. The Black-owned and Black-centered table. I was about to continue by when I paused slightly. This person looked a bit familiar, but I was a little too far away. Okay, I'll move a little closer, but not in an awkward way. I scooted in just a little bit more to make out a face. And there he was. Ethan, sitting at that table. *What the fuck*?

Not like there was anything wrong with him wanting to eat wherever or with whomever he wanted. But this shit was highly unusual. Like extremely suspicious. Out of all of my White friends, including Jacq, he was the LAST person I would expect at that table. I saw then that he was sitting next to our mutual friend, so that made a little bit more sense. However, those two were not close because they never spent lunch together... *Why the hell was Ethan there?* And then I experienced a weird emotion. It was similar but not all like losing track of a small child and finding them at the table with random people. I started to feel a bit possessive. He was my White person, dammit! Not theirs. That was messed up, but I was the main Black person he hung with. But more importantly, I wanted to know how he got to that table. There was no way in hell he just walked up to that table and sat down. He was not that extroverted. At all. Someone invited him to sit there, and for some reason, he agreed. So who was it? And what, pray tell, were they talking about? It looked like he was smiling and not visibly uncomfortable, or maybe he was masking it. And at one point, we did lock eyes. I saw him, and he saw that I saw him. I was not confident enough to walk over, but I did give him a confused look. But at that moment, another Black individual locked eyes with me and got confused and a little upset, as if he thought I was staring at him. *Move, fool, I wasn't looking at you! Forget it,* I thought, and I walked away.

I didn't bring it up later, and in true White avoidant fashion, neither did he. I became very suspicious of the Black folk. My thoughts went dark enough to assume they invited him to discourage him from hanging out with me. I don't know why I had that thought. These folks were nice people, and they have not given me any prior indication that they would sabotage my friendship. Maybe it wasn't the friendship I was worried about. But no one knew the feelings I was struggling with. The atypical love-ish that lived in between the margins. To the average outsider, I was part of a friend group with Ethan and his girlfriend. That was a well-known fact. So why did I fear them telling him not to become anything but a friend? The only inkling of a notion I could come up with was a previous conversation about interracial attraction and relationships at one of the Black student group meetings. I was one of the very few I attended, but it left a weird impression on me. For one, I was surprised at how many people did not favor dating outside their race. I guess I shouldn't say that. I'm not sure if many of them were against the idea, so much as there was much conversation about the importance of interracial dating. The importance of Black love. Which is a great and great and a beautiful thing. Too often, Black relationships are portrayed in society and the media as toxic, painful, and full of drama. However, the emphasis on Black love made me question what they thought about experiences beyond that. And for that reason, I became nervous about how they felt about my friendships and spending time with White people.

I may not have been popular, but if folks knew of me, it was the fact that I did not spend nearly as much time with the Black folks as I did with my White friends. Frankly, I didn't give a fuck about what they thought about my spending time with other people from other races, with the notable exception of this predicament. I became self-conscious of their views about me and, more importantly, what information they were relaying to Ethan and if he would believe whatever they said and start avoiding me. Avoid getting closer to me and deepening our friendship to whatever the hell I wanted in this "in-between." And that terrified me. To this day, I have no idea what happened at the Black table. And I wished I dared to ask back then. I wished Ethan dared to tell me or at least assure me we were alright. But why did I need that type of validation and comfort from him? For him to tell me that he still cared for me? Sounds like something a girlfriend would want. And because I wasn't that, I guess I felt I didn't deserve those needs to be met.

Chapter Seventeen // Dialectics, Reimagined

Dialectics: opposing forces that can exist and be true simultaneously. A term that has been popularized into wellness modules of mindful living by a deeply intelligent woman with a dark, harrowing past who was able to overcome her struggles and lay the foundation for a model that would help millions of people in similar situations. A woman whose name was faintly reminiscent of a 1970s sitcom character, distinguished by her quirky love for acronyms. Her story was not at all like mine. This term did not apply to my life, not exactly. Yet, it had a faint and familiar aura that lingered like an extra on the background of the show that was my life. A Black woman's reimagining of the term goes as follows: opposing forces that reveal hard truths vital in understanding the complexities of one's life and essence of being. The recipient of these opposing truth forces would have reactions similar to micro-aggressions: disbelief, dissociation, shame, and confusion. However, micro-aggressions are outside forces meant to harm the individual. In contrast, these dialectics are not a product of racial degradation but are simply meant to reveal deeper, uncomfortable meaning in oneself. The old version of dialectics did not wholly apply to me, so I flipped it and reinterpreted it. A right kind of appropriation, I would add, lest I get canceled for it. Oh well. I was introduced to several me-dialectics throughout college, yet I had no idea what they meant. All I knew was that it terrified me subconsciously.

At a certain point, I could no longer withstand the ongoing, underlying tension between Jacq and me, especially when we lived together. So I did the only logical thing I could think of: created space between us. I never directly communicated to Jacq the reasons for not wanting to live in the same building. If I did that, it would mean articulating the problems that Jacq would never acknowledge were happening. What would be the point in doing all that work just to be gaslit again? No, thank you. I still don't know how I got it to work out, but somehow I was able to devise a reason that made sense to everyone on the outside. I said I was not comfortable or ready to leave the dorms and rent an apartment. It may have been an odd choice, but not unreasonable. I knew one thing for certain: by making that choice, I would be losing time with Ethan during our last year in college. The distance between his new apartment off-campus and my dorm was already far, and even further than the closer apartment that Jacq moved into. Distanced by choices.

After I admitted to myself the potentially deeper feelings I had for Ethan, a new set of thoughts entered my consciousness and lingered. I loved him, yet I also wanted him to be happy, even if it did not include me in the picture. I was so confused the moment I had these thoughts. It was hard enough for me to accept I had these in-between love feelings in the first place, and now I was confused by this new compulsion of selflessness. I could accept I wanted someone I cared about to be happy, but I did not understand why I appeared to be willing to give up my happiness in the process. How could I, as a feminist, reckon with this belief of sacrificing my happiness for someone else? I was acutely aware of the history of women having to suppress their needs and desires for the sake of other people's happiness, particularly men. I did not want to be another person who was part of that painful history of sacrifice. I didn't want to be the strong Black woman forced to put other people's needs in front of her own once again. That was so painful to think about; it angered me.

Yet, there was another layer to this predicament. We may be more than friends, but we were not lovers, and in this limited dichotomy of relationships, there was no space for me to exist. It was as if a part of me was already willing to accept the sad reality that my feelings could not exist openly in a world that prioritized romantic relationship love over anything else. So it was better in a sense to let go of the notion and to wish my recipient happiness in his path to receive the type of love that society accepted. And there was another part of me that did not want to give up hope, that wanted to continue to exist in the in-between, the multiplicity of love and feelings where she so comfortably thrived, albeit invisible. That was a strength I was willing to hold on to. But did I deserve it if it involved being in the middle of another romantic relationship? I did not believe my desires were necessarily disruptive to a romantic relationship; it was just another type of relationship existing at the same time. Those opposing parts of me would vary and intensity day by day. I still don't know who the winner is.

Time passed, and it became a bit more normal to not have Ethan appear so frequently in my life. I was also heavily preoccupied with schoolwork and other related responsibilities. On the days and weekends we did meet up, at an apartment hang with the rest of the squad and my new dorm mates, there was an instant reconnection. A spark reignited us when we locked eyes as I entered the room. A wave of peace and calm rolled over me. I was always nervous before these meetups, thinking it would be awkward, but as soon as he looked at me and smiled as I entered his place, all of those fears washed away. It was as if no time had passed. It was magical and shameful at the same time. That thought of letting go and wanting him to be happy in his relationships kept creeping up in my mind. As I think back now, I guess I never gave a thought to the alternative: perhaps Ethan's version of happiness always included me in it. That thought never occurred to me.

One night, the guys threw a party, which turned into an unintentional mini-reunion with former floor mates. It was good to see the folks that came. Surprisingly, one of our RAs also showed up, someone who had since graduated. He was in "the real world," and it surprised me that he would want to come back and socialize with us, little people. It was premature thinking, I know. I was chilling with my core squad, watching them play beer bong, the grossest of college games, when our old RA walked up to us.

"Hey!" he said enthusiastically.
"Yo!" we said, super chill, cause, *whatevs.*

He stood back, watching us play, reminiscing about our time together. He talked about all the pranks he used to play on us, including that one time he straight-up just blasted a fart right in my face. Wow, I sure missed that.

Partway through our chat, Ethan walked away to grab something in the kitchen. It was just Jacq, me, and our lovely ex-RA at the moment. No, seriously, he was a great, kind person. It's just his sense of humor didn't always resonate with me. I mean, every time I think of him, I couldn't not think of him farting in my face. Even today, which is hilarious.

"So you and Ethan are still dating?" He asked Jacq.
"Yup, still going strong," she said, slightly sarcastic. She was clearly annoyed by the phrasing.
"Yeah." He paused. He looked right at me.
"I thought you and Ethan would end up together."
Silence.

Now, there are things you hear and things you think you hear. He made that comment at a volume that was not too soft, but not very loud. Whatever it was, it made me question what I heard. I was very unsure of what I heard. Lovely readers and listeners, you can all probably guess that he did say those words. Here was my thought process during that night:

What did he say? Did he say what I think he said? That doesn't make sense. There's no way he could say that. Maybe I should ask him to repeat it. But I hate having to ask folks to repeat stuff; it makes me look stupid and appear like I wasn't paying attention. What a bad guest that would make me. And what if I do ask him, and he does repeat what I thought I heard? That would make things worse. Jacq wouldn't like that. Wait, why isn't Jacq saying anything? Oh shit, I really don't know what he said. Okay, maybe I won't say anything and smile. Yeah, that's good. I really don't know what else to do here.

My mind was churning in confusion. I could not believe that our former RA would say something like that. What I was thinking, deep inside, was that I could not believe anyone in this world would think about Ethan and me as a couple. I struggled with knowing what Jacq thought about us, but that was the extent of it. I never considered other people's perceptions of us outside the squad, let alone someone who appeared to be secretly rooting for us. Fuck. That sounds too cocky of me. I don't want this tale to sound like a Twilight Team Jacob or Team Edward situation. And who would I be in that scenario? I guess Jacob? I'm not a pasty White person, so…

Needless to say, my choice of smiling in silence did not help things. And in pure White fashion, Jacq kept her silence, and she eventually changed the subject. How the hell do White women do that? And both me and our former RA, who are both non-White, had no choice but to follow along and act as nothing happened.

Dialectics. Maybe other people noticed more about Ethan and me than I realized. *But what did that mean?* I could not believe it. It was a non-relationship, and he was in a real relationship. Looking back, I know there was more to this. I could not believe that folks would consider that Ethan, a White man, would be interested in a relationship with me, a Black woman. No, that's not quite it. I can believe it. I have seen countless interracial attractions and relationships prior to and during college, although it was much less frequent in college. I think what I could not truly believe was that I would have the power to shake the foundation of a White romantic relationship. That someone would be interested in leaving that relationship...for me. And that had to be inherent in my Blackness, or how I thought other people viewed MY Blackness compared to others, even those in interracial relationships. All of these things can be true at the same time. Fuck dialectics.

Let us not forget the biggest dialectic of them all: the relationship between Jacq and me. Wow, it was filled with so many contradictions, so many opposing forces; yet in those cases, those forces revealed themselves to be hard contradicting truths. I never knew how to characterize Jacq. I still don't. One belief that kept coming back to me throughout my life was that she was NOT the villain in my story. Y'all are probably thinking, "REALLY?" Yeah, really. I don't want to hold onto hate. Sure, there were aspects to our relationship that were highly toxic; I do not deny that. And she did hurt me over and over again, and so did I. I can admit that there were things that I may have done to hurt her feelings. And this is not me giving grace to a White woman for the sake of Whiteness if that makes sense. I do not want to lean into the socialized, problematic narrative of being protective of a White woman over my well-being. I will not put myself down for the sake of uplifting Whiteness over my own lived experiences. Fuck that noise. And if you don't understand that noise, do your research.

There are subtle, nuanced differences to the following beliefs, and all can exist at the same time. You can love someone. They can hurt you. Black women and White women can be friends. Black women and White women can be enemies. I cared for Jacq, and she hurt me. Jacq cared for me, and I hurt her. You can be a good person and do terrible things. We loved Ethan in our ways, but we didn't know what love truly was at that time. I loved Jacq, but I can't pinpoint the parts I loved. Or I knew the parts I loved, but I was too embarrassed to admit it. I guess I already did. Maybe that's the point. You can love someone and not know why, or the reasons don't make sense. That's an internal reckoning for me and no one else. I don't need your approval, but I desperately want you to understand me.

Chapter Eighteen // The Last Night

Queerplatonic. It's a word I would hear for the first time several years after I finished college. And it took another couple of years before I finally understood what it meant. Damn you, AVEN! Where were you when I needed it? Well, I guess you were still in your early stages in the internet world, and truth be told, I probably wouldn't have sought you out even if you were well known at that time. That doesn't apply to me, I would think. The hell it didn't. I can't relate to that label: I'm a sexual being. The hell it doesn't relate. I've always existed in the in-between when it came to relationships. I felt a desire and a connection in places that technically "should not exist." But who are we to let others define our desires and connections? Who are we to say that meaningful connections only exist in friendships or relationships? Who are we to say that we can only be completely sexless or completely sexual? That we cannot experience sensuality without sexuality and have affection and connection with folks outside of relationships? Many folks may not get me, but I refuse to believe I am the only one who feels and lives like this.

I wanted everything that day, graduation day, to go smoothly. I was strongly inclined to ensure I had a proper goodbye with everyone. Well, almost everyone. I wasn't sure if Jacq even wanted to say goodbye or if she was planning to ruin even that. So I avoided thinking about her and focused on everyone else. And I did get my wish, almost. It may sound weird, but I never got to properly say goodbye to Joaquin, and I kind of regret that. I could not, for the love of me, locate that man on that day. I may have been jealous of him, but he was still a cool dude. Oh, Joaquin, where art thou now?

I wanted to save the biggest ones for the night. I haven't mentioned this much, but after I stopped living near Jacq, I did develop new friendships with other floor mates, some of whom overlapped living with Jacq and me. So I did spend more time with them and less time with Jacq during our last year. I wanted to make time to say goodbye to new-ish friends, along with Ethan. I must spare some time for Ethan. I was so adamant about making a proper goodbye that I did not drink that night or not that much. I never really drank to begin with, but even I was interested in drinking during my graduation, especially since I was 21 and my parents could not give me SHIT about it. Ha, I was legal, and I can drink in front of you! At least, that thought was in my mind, as I sipped a little bit of my large margarita during our family dinner that evening. Just a little bit before I said to myself: "That's enough! I don't want to get too tipsy and forget the rest of the night." I'm such a fucking nerd.

I need to take several steps backward and discuss a recent factor that impacted my outlook for the night. The day before, I met up with another freshman-year friend, Amy, whom I had not seen in a while. We got along great, but we lost connection over the years. She was there during Jacq and Ethan's awkward courtship, and she would be the one ten years later who told me they were married during our reunion night. Needless to say, she always had the tea, and ten years ago was no exception. During our little meetup, she told me that she had a conversation with Jacq, and Jacq told her that she was considering breaking up with Ethan.

WHAT?? I didn't know that was an option for Jacq. She held on to this man for all these years. I thought she would be the last person to think about breaking up. But lo and behold, the hot gossip was that Jacq felt that Ethan was becoming too clingy, and she needed space. This blew my mind. *Was she going to break up with him before or after graduation? If she did, what would that mean for Ethan and me? Should I take my shot? And what shot, exactly?* I wanted to be with him, but once again, it wasn't entirely in the way that he was with Jacq. I wanted for me to exist in the picture with Jacq or without her, but not replacing her. The two were different.

That last night of college was perhaps the most painful in my life. I broke up with someone whom I never went out with. No one talks about that type of loss. No one wants to acknowledge that loss. He was more than a friend, but not a sexual partner. It was still a real relationship. I'm not a fan of zucchini, but I've grown to love butternut squash over the years, so I'll use that term instead.

I invited Ethan and Jacq over to my suite and some other mutual friends from my older and newer squads. The cool part was that we all knew each other, so it wasn't awkward. He came over surprisingly fast, almost eager to see me. He said that Jacq was on her way, which I interpreted as she was never coming. For a few hours, it appeared that I was correct.

We all started together, and slowly, people split into smaller groups... Before that happened, I was in a group of three, including Ethan, and we talked about keeping in contact after college. The big elephant in the room. He didn't seem to like the idea of social media, but that was the last stitch I had to keep him in my life. Soon enough, it was just the two of us in my room. *Should I take my shot?*

"Can we keep in touch on Facebook?" I asked him again.

"I don't know. You know, I don't use it that often. I don't like it." That part was true. He wasn't lying. He never did use social media. But then I thought about the previous time I tried texting him over break and how he didn't respond. *Was that part of Jacq's doing, or his lack of awareness?* I didn't want to turn into that jealous person who sent that angry text again, yelling at him for not responding. It was an ugly time for me, to get so angry that I cursed through text: "*You asshole! I guess I am not as important of a person to keep in contact with as your girlfriend*!" Yeah, I fucking said that. I think a part of me dissociated after that moment, in disbelief that I would

177

be so direct. But years later, I remembered writing that message. I did respond a little while afterward that night, stating that I was sorry, and he forgave me, but we never did talk about what it meant for me to say that. And that was the time right before my birthday when I received that awful cake that I thought was from Jacq. I put the pieces together later that maybe he was planning to surprise me with the cake to mend things, but Jacq got in the way. So I was conflicted: What were my other options if I couldn't keep in touch with him via text or Facebook?

I told him plainly, in perhaps the most painfully honest moment in my life:

"I don't know what to do here. I don't know if I can stay friends with someone on Facebook if they won't respond to my messages." I said "friends on Facebook," but it was clear between the lines. I needed some reciprocation on social media or in real life; if I wasn't getting it, that was it for me... Even back then, I knew enough to advocate for my desires, whether or not they were socially acceptable.

He nodded in agreement with my sentiment, his head slightly down. There was something different yet the same about him that night. If he truly wanted to avoid me that night, did not care about me, and no longer wanted to speak with me, he could have not stopped by my dorm and walked into my room that night. He could have ignored my text message and made an excuse not to come. It would be a super-easy way to not say goodbye in person and end things since I was flying out the next morning. But here he was: sitting in silence in my bedroom, just the two of us. But he didn't make an effort to ensure a path for us in the future. Maybe this was truly our goodbye, *forever.*

Then that thought came up again: I wanted him to be happy, even if it didn't include me. This time, it hit differently. There was no denying it. The path that I wanted to take with him was not happening. And I didn't want to hate him for it. I could never tell what he was thinking: if he wanted me in his life but was too afraid to say it. If he missed me before I was even gone. If he cared for me in ways that I never knew. None of that mattered. Deep down in my heart, and much to my dismay, I knew that night it would be the last time I would see him. And with that, I was willing to accept that I did want him to be happy. Even if I disagree with this whole situation, even if I wanted things to be better for us. Something inside me wanted to scream: "Fight for me! Fight for us. I can't be the only one who feels this way. I can't be the only one who is trying. I know you care about me." That part shocked me. All this time, I kept denying his feelings about it. There was part of me that thought it was true, that he did love me, whatever that meant, but my low self-image had previously prevented me from believing it. Not on this night. Why was he in my room? He cared for me in a way that existed beyond societal understanding and between us. Yet, he stood still.

It didn't matter. Those feelings did not matter when faced with the harsh reality. A choice was made. In the end, I wanted him to be happy, even if it didn't include me. Maybe I was a sucker for taking the high road, but even back then, I knew I didn't want to hold on to hatred and contempt. My past taught me all too well about the side effects of that path. This situation wasn't the same. Those folks hated me. They bullied me. I kept wrestling with the idea of whether or not Ethan liked me. Whether he was just being nice. But why was he in my room that night? Alone with just me? Against my self-loathing and disbelief, that must have meant something.

Later on that night, Jacq did stop by for a few minutes. Can you believe it? Anyway, her arrival meant Ethan's exit, so I was too deflated to be annoyed by her fashionable lateness. Her arrival meant Ethan's exit; her appearance was more of a signal to wrap things up. In the minute before they left, she turned to face me with her arms wide open as if to signal a request for a hug? What? I couldn't believe my eyes. Once again, I wasn't sure it was genuine.

"Really?" I said out loud in disbelief in front of everyone.

"Okay." I then leaned in for a church hug, you know, the one with your booty sticking out and your arms too far away to do a normal wrap-around-the-shoulders hug. Super distant.

The people around us stood wide-eyed, shaking their heads. It looked like they could not believe I openly called her out for what would be the last time. A great goodbye, I thought, as they walked away. I was going to lie firmly on that hill of authenticity and integrity, even if it killed me. Even if it was the last thing, I said. Ethan knew what I wanted and where I stood with him, and Jacq knew where she stood with me. The truth of the matter is that deep down, I was connected to Jacq. I will only say this once: I may have loved her. And feel free to take that in whatever way you want. Yet, in that place of *schadenfreude*, it meant that everyone saw that sour moment. A moment I wished didn't have to happen the way that it did.

And that was the last time all three of us were in the same room together.

Epilogue

After crying that summer and feeling sad for a few years, the pain became duller. After that last night, I almost immediately deleted them from my socials, so I had no idea where their lives took them. It may have been harsh, but I could not bear to witness their life growth without being there to enjoy it with them. Ten years and 3790 miles later, here I am. They say time heals wounds, and to some extent, it was true for me. It clarified how different we all were as people and the motives behind people's actions, including mine. Over the years, I went on an unintentional journey of learning more about Whiteness. I will say to the folks that I would consider my allies were people I knew around those college times, and not as much when I became older. I knew that back then as I do now. I miss folks engaging with my bluntness and authenticity, no matter how awkward it was. I wonder if I could have that "Black people on the radio" conversation with White folks nowadays. Well, it would depend on where you live. And the recent racial reckoning, unfortunately, drove more people in certain parts of the country into a weird combination of urgent badgering for answers followed by silence when it actually mattered. Nothing tires you faster than people catching up to acknowledge things that have been happening forever, y'all. Then not committing to the work or cultivating the meaningful relationships needed to make change. Once again, the intensity depends on where you live. I guess?

We *tired*.

I see Ethan now and again in my dreams. Sometimes it's the three of us sitting on the couch chatting with our friends. When it's the two of us, I imagine we're either in the past or in some imagined future where we are catching up, talking about where we ended up geographically and with our careers. Then there are times when I am actively searching for him: sometimes I find him, and sometimes I don't. And many other times, Jacq is there, either just with me or all three of us, replaying the second-hand love triangle. Fighting, crying, laughing, rejoicing. Recreating every type of drama-filled scenario I can imagine. Sometimes it's just the two of us walking around campus or in our dorms laughing. Other times, we are a happy throuple tribe. Something beyond and between romance and friendship. Just existing in peace and calm. Where they love me just as openly as I love them. Those are the times when I'm least confused and not affected by guilt.

In the depths of my mind, in a world with openness and no limitations, I imagine a life of community. Where we would grow together and celebrate the wealth of life's vast experiences and milestones. Where I would be to both of them: a more-than-friend, supporter, auntie, companion, confidant, part of the village.

"Maybe one day, we'll meet again and explain to each other what really happened. Maybe one day, we'll finally understand. Until then, I hope you live your best life, and I hope you really do all the things you always wanted to do." r.m. drake @rmdrk

I cried inside my mind the night of our non-reunion, the tears unable to pour out and fall down my face. I rarely cry about things, and this was just another one of those times. I felt sad for what felt like years, but it only lasted several weeks. Then, my life moved on.

Forgiveness is so fucking hard, especially for yourself. I thought of myself as a villain for too many years, as if my desires at that time were reprehensible. Now I know there could have been space for everyone; it just would have looked different from the norm. But what is the norm anyway? I wish I could tell you that I completely let go of my self-hatred. I was able to let go of the excess anger surrounding those past events, which was not easy for me. As much as I learned to embrace anger as a signal for self-compassion and demand for well-deserved justice, I also used it sometimes as a vehicle towards changing things that were outside of my control, like people's personalities and past lived experiences, which was not helpful. I am more in a place of real peace.

"I'll never regret someone that I had an amazing time and experience with. Even if we fall off. You made my life special at a certain time. We grew together, even if we grew apart.
Thank you," @star.poets

Book Acknowledgements and Resources

This book is dedicated to those people who continue to authentically exist and thrive outside of societal expectations, to those who continue to challenge systems and ideologies by *speaking the truth*.

I also dedicate this book to my parents and sister: my biggest cheerleaders and bullshit detectors. I would not be where I am and who I am without their support. Thank you.

Shout out to my fellow alums from the Center of Human Sexuality Studies at Widener University, particularly those who have helped shaped my understanding of Black sexuality, gender, the impact systems of oppression, and our ongoing quest for liberation and pleasure. This list is not exhaustive but includes the important work of Ericka Hart, M.Ed., Tracie Q. Gilbert, PhD, Lexx Brown-James, PhD", PhD, Donna Oriowo, PhD, Tanya Bass, PhD and Cindy Lee Alves, M.Ed.

I hope this book can contribute complexity
to the ever-growing discourse.

IG Accounts

Seher @rehes
R.M. Drake @rmdrk
@star.poets
Yasmin Benoit @theyasminbenoit

Books

Refusing Compulsory Sexuality by Sherronda J. Brown

Ace by Angela Chen

Speech: "The Master's Tools Will Never Dismantle the Master's House" by Audre Lorde

Mental Health and Wellness

Dr. Jennifer Mullan @decolonizingtherapy

Thérèse Cator @embodiedblackgirl

Megan Thee Stallion: badbitcheshavebaddaystoo.com

National Suicide Prevention Hotline: text or call 988

If you or someone you know is suffering from body image issues, consider these resources:

The Body is Not an Apology by Sonya Renée Taylor

Health at Every Size by The Association for Size Diversity and Health (ASDAH)

Sonalee Rashatwar, IG: @thefatsextherapist